THE SHADOW OF ISIS

Also by Joel S. Zarley:

Chasing the Light
eBook Publication for Training

THE SHADOW OF ISIS

BY JOEL S. ZARLEY

PURPLE PALM MEDIA
COLUMBUS, OHIO MMXII

The Shadow of Isis

ISBN-13: 978-0-9826523-5-0
ISBN-10: 0-9826523-5-6

www.purplepalmmedia.com
Email: editor@purplepalmmedia.com

Printed in the United States of America

To my childhood friends, Dee Dee and Julie who are still with me today.

TRUTH UTTERED BEFORE ITS TIME IS
ALWAYS DANGEROUS.

—*Mencius (Chinese philosopher, 372-289 BC)*

CHAPTER 1

Grand Canyon, Arizona (March 1909)

The sun beat down without mercy on the small wooden boat as it slowly navigated through the Colorado River. It was technically still late Winter, yet it already felt to Kincaid like the heat of July. He looked up at the four thousand feet of sheer cliff face surrounding him. He was not positive, but he thought he could see snow coating the rim of the canyon nearly one mile above him. His eyes returned to the river, and the delicate navigation he must perform to avoid crashing onto one of the many rocks that lay in the rushing water in front of him.

He had started his journey on the water in the Green River near Vernal, Utah. Once in the Green River he journeyed slowly southward until he met the confluence of the Colorado. From there he headed southwest, until he was deep with the canyon. Gerald Edward (known as G.E. by most acquaintances) Kincaid had lost track of exactly how long he had been on this river journey, but he knew that the time measured in weeks at this point. Early in the journey he thought he might freeze to death, but now heat and sun caused him discomfort.

He had not intended to begin an epic journey down the river and into the Grand Canyon. But, then again, he had never intended to find himself in Vernal either. He had run off to one of the few towns in Utah not founded and controlled by the Mormons, after an unfortunate business deal with the church in Salt Lake City had gone south. Despite the calm and polite demeanor of the Mormons, Kincaid knew that they did not take well to being cheated in business. Technically, Kincaid believed he hadn't actually cheated the Mormons—sometimes a deal just goes bad and people lose their investment. Still, he thought it valuable to his own well being if he put as much distance between himself and The Great Salt Lake as possible.

He spent just a few days in Vernal. Despite the abundance of saloons and friendly women, he knew that his options were limited there. He ended up winning a boat in a crooked poker game, and thought it best to take his new bounty and flow out of town with the river.

Calling his winning a "boat" might be an overly

generous description. It was nearly twenty feet long, and about eight feet wide, and constructed entirely from wood. (Of which, about one third had the beginnings of pretty severe wood rot.) There was a small cabin built into the back third of the craft that was just large enough for a cot and a small stove. Kincaid thought it looked like a shack hastily built on a poorly constructed raft.

But, it would get him out of town, and that is all Kincaid cared about right now. He had heard rumors about recent gold discoveries in the Grand Canyon, and thought this sounded like as good of a plan as any. Maybe this would finally be the venture that paid off for him. God knows he was due. It seemed like no matter where he went, or what he did, things never worked out the way he planned. Just like the latest experience with the Mormons…

It never quite seemed fair. Even the times when he was playing by the rules and completely legal, he would still end up getting screwed on a deal. It didn't seem like the right kind of life for the first white child ever born in Idaho…

He smiled to himself when he thought of that. Actually, he wasn't even sure he was the first white child in Idaho. In fact, he knew it was pretty damn well impossible. But, that is what his daddy always told him—him and everyone else that would listen. Kincaid senior found early on that the fictional story of his son's birth was always worth a free drink or two.

Of course, the man he called his daddy really wasn't. William Kincaid was Gerald's mother's second husband. His real daddy had died in a Union prison during the war between the states. He had been found guilty of treason for supplying aid and comfort to the enemy. Technically, he had *sold* aid and comfort to the enemy, but that fact had held a very fine shade of difference for Mr. Lincoln's government.

Gerald had not been quite two years old when his biological father died, and his mother married Kincaid not quite a month later. His stepfather had always been good to him; treating him like he was his own son. He had never formally adopted the boy, but had given him his name anyway. Kincaid had been an alcoholic and a con man, but he had never raised a hand to Gerald or his mother. After his mother died of the consumption when he was twelve, his stepfather never even once considered abandoning the boy.

G.E. wasn't sure when the elder Kincaid came up with the story about him being the first white child born in Idaho, but he told it from the time the young boy could remember. After a while, Gerald began believing it himself and he continued the tradition. And the free drinks that went with it.

At almost 47 years of age, he was now the same age as his stepfather when he died, and nearly five years older than his birth father. He had promised himself that he would never die rotting in jail like his father. He might drink himself to death like daddy Willy (as he had affectionately called his stepfather), but he would never die as another man's prisoner. That's why he always kept moving; always just a few days ahead of whatever trouble he had caused most recently.

The rapids cleared, and Kincaid reached a rather calm pool in the river. He sat down on the hard wooden deck of the boat and wiped his sweaty brow. He put his hand inside his jacket, and felt the cool metal of his flask. It was nearly empty, but it would have to do for now. He had some more whiskey packed away in the cabin, and he could retrieve it when he stopped for the night.

He leaned his head back and took a deep swig from his flask. As he looked up, he saw a bright flash several hundred feet up from the canyon floor. He put the flask down and stared up at the cliff face, convinced the whiskey, the sun, and his mind were playing tricks on him. He stared for several minutes, and just when he was convinced it was nothing, he saw the flash again. G.E. Kincaid was not an educated man, but he knew a few things about the world. And one of the things he knew was that valuable things tended to shine.

He guided the boat over to a wide sandy area on the bank of the river. He hopped off and grabbed the front end of the boat and pulled it as far as he could onto the river bank. The last thing he needed was to lose his only means of transportation to this wretched river.

He found a small telescope packed away in one of the boxes in the boat's cabin, and used it to peer into the direction where he saw the glint of light. The combination of the poor quality of the spyglass and the glare of the sun made it difficult to see well, but he could make out what looked to be an opening in the cliff face. It appeared to be a cave, but the opening seemed almost purposeful; more of an arched doorway than some naturally occurring hole.

It looked like it would be a steep climb up to the cave opening. His eyes scanned the area near the bottom of the canyon and noticed that there were a series of setbacks in the rocks that meandered up toward the cave. While not exactly a trail, it would none-the-less provide a path to his desired destination without requiring him to scale the face of the cliff walls.

He grabbed a canteen of water, a lantern, a pickaxe and a small length of rope. Not exactly mountain climbing equipment, but it was the best he had and it would have to do. He put on an extra shirt over his current one to help protect him from any jagged rocks he may encounter, and he set off on his quest.

Over the next two hours he scaled the steep path.

At a few points in the journey the ledge he was following narrowed to just a few inches wide. During these times he would flatten his chest against the cliff as tightly as possible, and hugging the wall inch himself slowly along the path. Several times he was grateful for the fact that he did not possess a greater than normal fear of heights. Still, he consciously tried not to look down at the river flowing hundreds of feet below him.

Finally, he made it to a ledge about one hundred feet wide by twenty feet deep. He had no way of actually measuring, but he figured this ledge must be at least five to six hundred feet above the canyon floor. A large arched passage lay at the deepest part of the ledge, leading into the cliff wall. It appeared much larger at this vantage point than it had from river level. From here, he guessed that the arched entry was at least twenty feet tall, and about eight feet wide.

He lit his lantern and peered into the entry way. He could only see a few feet inside, but there appeared to be some sort of walkway that sloped downward into the cave. He swallowed hard and looked around him.

"Well, shit, G.E.," he said to himself. "The gold ain't gonna come find you."

He slowly began walking into the cave. Once inside the archway, the interior opened into a much larger room. The light from the lantern did not travel too far, but he could tell that the interior space was massive. Instead of traveling straight in and deeper into the cavern, he decided to find the side walls and work his way around from the outside edges. That would make it easier to systematically sweep the room searching for valuables. It would also allow him to retrace his steps along to the wall to find his way out quickly, if for some reason that should become necessary.

Even with the lantern, he only had about ten feet of visibility in any direction. Starting from the entry, he began heading left staying close to the front wall at all times. He began to count out the paces that he had walked. When he reached one hundred and sixty two paces, he saw the first corner of the room. He directed the lantern to the parallel wall, and saw an image painted in red:

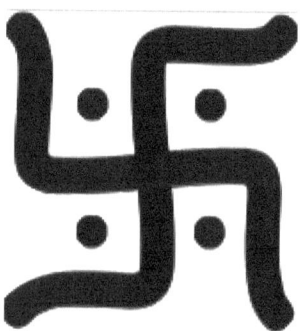

He was not familiar with the symbol, but figured if someone had gone to all the trouble of getting up here to paint it on a wall, it must be important. He thought it resembled an odd shaped letter X.

"X marks the spot, I guess," he said out loud, his voice echoing off the stone walls. He was startled by the reverberating echo throughout the cavernous space. "Christ," he said in a now near whisper.

He continued to slowly move his way around the edges of the room. He was about twenty feet from the painted image on the wall when he encountered gold for the first time. But, it was not gold like he expected. Instead of finding a few nuggets embedded into a wall, he stumbled upon an gold figure that was a full head taller than himself.

He gasped at first, thinking that he had encountered another person in this dark cave. Then, he realized what he was actually seeing. It was a statue in the shape of a person, but made entirely out of gold.

He looks like a damn Oriental, Kincaid thought to himself.

His mind spun with the possibilities. His first thought was how much it must be worth. His second thought was how much it must weigh, and how would he ever get it out of the canyon?

He figured he could worry about those details later—right now he was concerned with what other treasures might await him. And, there were a considerable number of other treasures. He found multiple large gold statues like the first one he found, as well as smaller versions ranging from several inches to a few feet high. He also found small jewelry-like pieces made of gold and silver and encrusted with jewels.

G.E. Kincaid felt like pinching himself to make sure he was not dreaming; or even worse—had crashed his boat against some rocks in the river, hit his head, and was imagining this whole scene. But, it was real. He had finally found the treasure that had eluded him all of his life. Gerald Edward Kincaid was finally going to have the life he deserved.

He was examining strange, writing-like markings on yet another gold statue when he heard a noise. It was very faint at first, but it slowly grew in volume. It was the sound of voices—he was sure of that. He could not understand what the voices were saying, since they seemed to be in some strange language he had never heard before. But after a few moments he was positive that's what he was hearing—coming from even deeper within the cavern. He felt the holster around his waist and realized for the first time that he had left his revolver on the boat.

Like most men who had spent the better part of their lives getting caught being in the wrong place at the wrong time, Kincaid's first reaction was to run. However, he kept his wits about him long enough to pocket several pieces of the gem encrusted jewelry, and one of the very small gold statues. He extinguished the lantern, and moved quickly as he followed the side wall back to the entrance of the cave.

The climb up to the ledge holding the cave had taken him nearly two hours, but he made the trip back down in about one-fourth that time. Not only was gravity working for him on the return trip, he was also feeding off the adrenalin of a man who feared he had stumbled into a situation way above his head.

He returned to the river bank in a near run, threw the items he carried with him onto the boat deck, and pushed the craft into the river. He jumped onto the boat at the last moment as the current pulled it into the stream.

He did not even notice that he had dropped his daddy's flask as he scurried onto the boat.

G.E. Kincaid had been drunk for the better part of two weeks.

After barely escaping the rapids of the river with his life, Kincaid abandoned the boat nearly immediately after getting out of the canyon. It was not that big of a loss—the boat had sustained quite a bit of damage during the journey, and probably would have never seen another voyage anyway.

After that, Kincaid had made his way down to Phoenix where he attempted to placate himself with whiskey and easy women.

Kincaid found that if he was drunk enough, he wouldn't have the dreams. Every night when he slept he would hear those same voices from the cavern. And, while he could never quite remember their message the next morning, he knew in his heart the things they told him were not pleasant.

As unpleasant as the dreams were, the thought that he had abandoned what could have been millions of dollars in treasure was even more haunting. He had tried to convince himself that maybe he had imagined the cave— that he hadn't really seen those things. But then, he would pull one of the small pieces from the stash he kept carefully hidden, and he knew that it was true. And, he feared that the thoughts of what he had lost would always torture him.

During those weeks he thought a lot about going back to retrieve the treasure. However, he realized there were two significant problems with that plan. First, the sheer volume of the treasure and its inconvenient position mid-way up the canyon would make it almost impossible to move. Secondly, he realized that he did not really remember the location of the treasure; he had been off one of many tributaries of the Colorado River when he stumbled upon the site. He had no idea how to return there.

The thoughts of the cavern and the treasure were

preoccupying his almost every thought. So, it was probably no surprise that under the fog of over a fifth of bourbon he decided to unburden himself.

Sitting in a bar on Central Avenue in downtown Phoenix he met a young man named Davis Evers. Evers was a young reporter with the Phoenix Gazette, one of the major daily newspapers serving the city. Evers was young and ambitious, but so far had been unsuccessful in distinguishing himself with the big scoop. That all changed the night he met G.E. Kincaid.

Kincaid could not remember later how he started telling Evers about his discovery in the Grand Canyon; or for that matter, how he even began talking to him at all. But soon, he had told him the entire story.

Of course, Evers had first thought the story was just the ramblings of an old drunk. But then, Kincaid had shown him the proof—the items he had taken from the cavern in the canyon. He had talked the old man into letting him take one of the smaller items to have it looked at by a history professor he consulted on stories at the Tempe Normal School. (Which many years later would be renamed Arizona State University.) He promised Kincaid he would return it after his professor friend had evaluated it.

Evers found Kincaid sitting in the same bar a few nights later, and told him that his professor friend had declared the article brought to him was at least three thousand years old, and was most likely Egyptian in origin. The professor was going to contact a former colleague at the Smithsonian Institution about a potential expedition.

Kincaid was upset that someone else might be trying to lay claim to his treasure. But, Evers convinced him that if he allowed him to print a story about the discovery, clearly crediting him with the find, he would be publicly protecting his rights to it.

A few days later, on April 5, 1909, the story ran on the front page of the Phoenix Gazette with the headline:

EXPLORATIONS IN GRAND CANYON
Mysteries of Immense Rich Cavern being brought to light;
Jordan is enthused; Remarkable finds indicate ancient people
migrated from Orient

Kincaid was quoted quite extensively in the article, which described his find of the cavern in vivid—if not somewhat exaggerated—detail. It mentioned his trip down the Green River, but failed to mention the recent unfortunate incident with the Mormons. He was also very pleased that the article described him as the "first white child born in Idaho." Daddy Willy would have been very proud. Overall, Kincaid came across as quite the heroic explorer.

The article also talked about an upcoming expedition by an archeologist from the Smithsonian named S.A. Jordan. Professor Jordan promised a full accounting of the contents of mysterious cavern. The majority of the treasure would eventually be displayed in the collections of the Smithsonian, but Evers had convinced Kincaid that he would be line for a handsome finder's fee. It would easily be enough money for him to live the rest of his life in comfort.

Things were looking up for G.E. Kincaid. He finally believed he was going to have the life he always believed he deserved. That was until late one night nearly two weeks after the Gazette story ran.

He had been asleep (or more accurately, passed out) in the rooming house he had been staying in since arriving in Phoenix. He startled to consciousness as his room door was kicked open. He sat up in bed to see a small group of Army officers, weapons drawn, standing inside his door.

"Mr. Kincaid? Mr. G.E. Kincaid?" one of the officers said.

"Ye-ye-yes," he stammered in return.

"Sir, we have a warrant for your arrest issued by Secretary of War Dickinson. We have orders to take you with us immediately."

Kincaid could not believe his ears; this made absolutely no sense to him. He tried to question the men as to why they were taking him, but after the brief explanation, they refused to speak any more. He tried to bolt for the door to escape, but was met with the butt of a shotgun to the back of his head.

After that he was handcuffed, and had a hood placed over his head. He was placed on a train with his captors, where they traveled all night and most of the rest of the next day. Finally, he was led off the train and into a cool, dank building. The hood was finally removed when he was placed in the prison cell.

He was in solitary confinement and completely alone except for the few minutes three times a day when his captors would bring him food and water. He only left the cell once a week to be taken to the shower room. For weeks he begged for some sort of explanation, but would receive nothing but silence. Eventually, he gave up even asking.

He lost complete track of time, and was convinced he was going mad. He found it harder and harder to breathe in the damp cell, and would wake up in a panic convinced he was drowning. He knew that he would not be able to take this much longer.

After an entire life promising himself that he would never allow himself to die in prison like his father, on October 1, 1909 G.E. Kincaid did precisely that.

CHAPTER 2

Grand Canyon, Arizona (Early April, Current Day)

The one man kayak slipped through the rapid with relative ease; compared to the last few he had navigated this was nothing—maybe a class three at best.

He had been kayaking, rafting, and sailing nearly his entire life. It was one advantage of having a father who was career military—they moved around a lot and he got exposed to a lot of different skills.

Mark Newman had left his campsite near the Phantom Ranch a few hours earlier. He had risen early, and left with the first full light of dawn. He had successfully fought the temptation to leave even earlier. Facing this river in any amount of darkness would have been a suicide wish.

He was in his third day on the Colorado, and he was ready for this part of the journey to be over. Not that he was unhappy to be here; he had been planning this trip for a long time. He had been submitting applications into the lottery to win one of the few permits for solo rafting through the Grand Canyon for the past three years. He only happened to get the permit this year because there had been a cancellation, and his name had been pulled from the waiting list.

Ideally, he would have made this trip in the Summer when the weather would have been more predictable. But, early Spring was better than no time at all. The one advantage to making this trip in April is that the river's tributaries were full from the melt of the Winter's snow pack.

He had not followed the normal route of rafters and kayakers exploring the Colorado River through the canyon. Of course, his reason for being here was significantly different than most tourists as well. While others came for the beauty of the river and the canyon, he was here for a much bigger purpose. He was here to find evidence of one of the world's greatest anthropological mysteries.

He had begun his river journey in the Little Colorado River in the heart of the Navajo Nation. He had started there for two primary reasons. First, because it allowed the easiest entry into the canyon without putting up with the throngs of tourists; but secondly because it gave him the opportunity to get the last bit of information he needed. He had spent the final night before beginning this journey on the Hopi

Reservation, in the company of one of the wisest women he had ever met.

After leaving camp this morning, he had abandoned the Colorado and entered Bright Angel Creek. From there he maneuvered through several smaller tributaries until making it to his current location. He had not seen another human being since shortly after leaving camp. He glanced down at his waterproof watch—it was 9:10 AM.

Ahead of him, he could see where the waterway narrowed to an opening of only about twenty feet between the canyon walls. A chain link fence stretched from one side of the stream to the other, its bottom only a few inches above the water, and its sides bolted into the cliff face. He could see a large sign bolted to the fence. The lettering on the sign was large enough that he could read it clearly even at over one hundred feet away. It read:

WARNING! RESTRICTED ACCESS
NO ENTRY
PROTECTED BAT HABITAT
U.S. PARKS SERVICE PERSONNEL ONLY
ALL TRESPASSERS WILL BE PROSECUTED

Mark smiled to himself.

"Yeah, right," he said out loud to no one in particular.

"I'm sure they're really worried about some bats."

He pulled the kayak over to the stream's edge along a narrow sandy shore just ahead of the fence. He got out of the boat and took off the life jacket he had been wearing for the past three days. Where he was going next, it would no longer be needed.

He reached into the storage area of the kayak in front of the seat and pulled out his stash of gear. He had purposely traveled light for this trip, but there were some supplies that were a necessity. He pulled out several one gallon water jugs he had stored in the front of the boat—you could never have too much drinking water in the desert. He poured the contents of two of the jugs into a backpack water reservoir he had purchased specifically for this trip. He also grabbed two large flashlights, and some very basic rock climbing paraphernalia he had been able to fit into the kayak. He also double-checked the bag to make sure his waterproof digital camera was present.

He turned on his satellite phone and glanced down at the battery indicator—it was down to thirty percent. He had significantly underestimated how quickly his new toy would run through a battery charge. He could kick himself for leaving the phone turned on during the first day on the river. But, what was done was done—he would have to deal with it, and hope for the best.

He began walking down the narrow shoreline toward the chain link fence. He looked around carefully. He could not see any evidence of security video cameras, but he knew they were here somewhere. If what he believed was true, this site was way too important for the government to leave unmonitored. He only hoped that he would have enough time to get the information he was seeking before the Feds caught up with him. Maybe when he told them that his sister was an FBI agent they would go easier on him…

He began scaling the cliff near the fence edge until he was high enough to clear the top of the fence. Luckily, it was only about twelve feet high. Once on the other side, he began scaling down the wall and dropped to the sandy ground. From here, he would have to walk for the next five miles or so—by his best estimation.

About ninety minutes later he reached his goal.

He looked up at the cliffs around him, and saw the target of the last few years of his work and life. After all this time, it seemed surreal to actually be standing here.

Most people would look up at these cliffs and never see what was really there. But, of course, that was all part of the design. He, however, knew what was there—he had spent a lot of time, money, and sleepless nights putting all of the pieces together.

The only thing that surprised him was how easy

it actually was to get to the entrance of the cave. He had counted on a pretty perilous climb, but there was practically a trail leading straight to the camouflaged entry. Granted, a difficult and pretty precarious trail, but a trail none-the-less.

The climb up to the ledge took him less than thirty minutes. He had been prepared for so much worse, this part of the trek actually seemed fairly easy by comparison. On the ledge he looked to the areas where the cliff met the ledge floor, and there he saw it—a projection device. His eyes followed to where the projection terminated. He fired up the larger flashlight and shone it on the terminus of the projection. Momentarily, he interrupted its illusion.

He walked into the cavern. To someone watching from a distance, it would have appeared that Mark Newman had walked directly through a solid rock wall.

Once inside he moved to the left, following the front wall of the cavern until he reached the first corner. He pointed the flashlight at the wall in front of him, and saw exactly what he had expected—a swastika. He momentarily thought about how this symbol might be perceived if someone stumbled onto it here, not fully understanding its rich history.

He continued walking deeper into the cavern. The first room was huge—and empty—but he knew there was even more. About five hundred yards in he pulled out his satellite phone and turned it on. There was no service. Apparently, even the satellite signal could not penetrate these dense stone walls.

Either that, or something's blocking it, he thought to himself.

He swallowed hard. He was trying hard not to let his fear get the best of him. But, standing here alone in the dark cavern, that was easier said than done.

He paused for moment and gathered his courage. Then, with a deep breath, he continued walking deeper into the chilly darkness.

CHAPTER 3

San Francisco, California (October 1951)

Julia Morgan sat back in her large leather desk chair and closed her eyes tightly. She was tired—more tired than she ever thought was possible. Throughout the 1920s and 1930s she had traveled up and down the California coast weekly, usually working six (or sometimes, seven) days a week. But now, even a simple morning in her office exhausted her.

Morgan was a small woman, well beyond what most would describe as petite. She was barely five feet tall, and her weight had never hit triple digits throughout her entire life. She opened her eyes and looked around. Her office in the Merchants Exchange Building had been her personal sanctuary for over forty years now, but for some reason it no longer looked the same.

She glanced over at her desk and saw the engraved

plaque commemorating her appointment of emeritus status in the American Institute of Architects. She had never asked for any other professional accolades, in fact, she had avoided notoriety at all costs. But, this particular honor she had actively sought. She believed she had earned the distinction, and very few of her peers would have disagreed.

Asking for this recognition was out of character for her, since she generally disdained any sort of publicity or attention. Throughout her long career she had refused to enter any competitions, write articles for professional journals, submit photographs to architectural magazines, or even serve on any committees with her colleagues. She openly dismissed such activities as appropriate only for "talking architects." She, as she would quietly explain, was a *working* architect.

She had served as William Randolph Hearst's personal architect for a large part of her career, and with him she believed she had done her best work. But even Hearst could not overcome her aversion to publicity, as one of his top magazine reporters, Adela Rogers St. John, would discover first hand.

In 1928, Miss St. John had contacted Julia Morgan for a *Good Housekeeping* article series she was writing on important American women. The reporter was flabbergasted by Morgan's refusal to even sit with her for an interview.

"But, Miss Morgan," she said crisply. "I have Mr. Hearst's permission."

"Well, then," Morgan had replied. "I suggest you interview Mr. Hearst."

Adela Rogers St. John wrote her article series on important American women, but the architect from San Francisco was never mentioned.

Julia Morgan was born in San Francisco in January, 1872 as the second child of Charles Bill Morgan and Eliza Woodland Parmelee Morgan. Charles Morgan abandoned a secure upper class life in New England to strike out on his own to make his fortune in mineral mining. Her mother came from similar stock, although of the Old South instead of New England. Julia's maternal grandfather had made his fortune dealing in cotton futures prior to the Civil War.

Charles Morgan was always considered somewhat of an adventurer, and shortly after his wedding he decided they should go where the new opportunities were available—and the land of opportunity was California. However, instead of taking the new transcontinental railroad across the country, Charles Morgan decided to sail around the tip of South America, exploring business opportunities as they went. Nearly eight months after leaving New York City, they sailed into the raw and rowdy frontier city of San Francisco.

They settled in a family hotel in the downtown area.

The couple's first child, a son they named Parmelee, was born in 1870. Julia was born two years later, and the family would eventually welcome three additional children over the subsequent years. The large family eventually moved to a big Victorian house in Oakland, where they would stay for the next fifty years.

Even with three sons, his second born was always Charles Morgans's favorite. He and his daughter were kindred sprits, sharing a love of engineering, art, and adventure. Morgan would often take his daughter with him on his various expeditions searching for new mineral strikes—an activity which greatly concerned her mother. For a woman with her Southern gentility, she did not believe it appropriate for a young lady to traipsing around mining camps. However, Parmelee had always been a sickly child so it was not feasible for him to accompany his father. So, while young Julia was out learning the mineral exploration business with her father, Parmelee stayed at home with his mother.

In fact, it was one of those those expeditions to the Grand Canyon when she was ten years old that she considered the single most defining event of her life.

In spite of traveling so much as a child and missing much school, Julia graduated in the top of her high school class. She went on to the University of California at Berkeley where she also graduated with honors in 1894 with a degree in civil engineering.

She wanted to mix her knowledge of mathematics and engineering with her love of art, and she believed the best place to pursue that goal would be at *L'Ecole des Beaux-Arts* in Paris, the premiere fine arts school in the world. There was only one problem—the school did not accept women.

For over two years she petitioned the school to admit women. Eventually, she was given the opportunity to take the entrance exams. To the school's dismay, she scored thirteenth highest out of 376 applicants. The school had no option but to accept her. Charles Morgan had never been so proud of his daughter.

After graduating from *L'Ecole des Beaux-Arts* she returned to San Francisco to begin her architectural career. She opened her first office in a small building on Montgomery Street which was completely destroyed in the great earthquake of 1906. After that she opened the office in the Merchants Exchange Building where she still was today.

She did some of her early work for her alma mater at Berkeley. It was through those projects that she met Phoebe Apperson Hearst, who was a major benefactor of the University of California. An early feminist and suffragist, she was impressed not only by Julia Morgan's work, but also how she had been instrumental in getting the *L'Ecole des Beaux-Arts* to change their policy on the admission of women.

Mrs. Hearst introduced the young female architect to her son, the newspaper tycoon William Randolph Hearst. The younger Hearst was also impressed by the woman's talent and commissioned her for several projects over their thirty-plus year association. The largest and most significant of which was their twenty eight year collaboration building *La Cuesta Encantada*—"the enchanted hill"—or as Hearst simply referred to it—"the ranch" in San Simeon. Everyone else, however, called it the Hearst Castle.

Over her long career she had designed over 700 buildings, including some of the most famous structures in California. But now, all that was over—she was finished. She called her assistant, Walter Hake, into her office.

Walter Hake had been with Morgan since very early in her career. He had been a construction supervisor on one of her first projects at Berkeley, and had been with her ever since. He had become a trusted colleague and a good friend.

"Walter," she said quietly, looking over her glasses. "I've decided to close down the office. It's time to retire."

Walter Hake nodded. In one way this did not come as a complete surprise to him. She was over eighty years old now, and he had noticed that his old friend and boss had started to slow down over the last few years. On the other hand, he never thought she would be a person to accept the fragility of old age.

"Well, ma'am, you've certainly had a good run. You've got a lot to be proud of—a lot to be proud about."

She smiled softly back at him.

"Thank you, Walter. I also want you to know how much I've appreciated your dedication and service over these many years. I've been putting something aside for your retirement as well…"

She slid a sealed white envelope across the desk to him. He picked it up and opened it. He had to look twice to make sure he was really seeing what he thought he was seeing. It was a check for one hundred thousand dollars.

"Oh, my, Miss Morgan," he said stammering. "I can't accept this."

"Don't be silly—of course you can. You have been an exemplary employee—and a good friend—for all these years. You deserve a comfortable retirement as well."

Walter fought hard to hold back the tear that was welling in his eye. He was going to miss this lady. He wondered what his wife would say when he told her that Miss Morgan had set them up for the rest of their lives. His wife had never much taken to Miss Morgan, but he thought this might go a long way to changing her opinion.

"Walter, there's one more thing I need you to do for me."

"Of course, Miss Morgan—anything."

"I want you to burn all of the office records. The blueprints, the files, my journals—everything."

"But, ma'am," he said, surprised at what she was saying. "Why would you want to do that? Those are important things—I'm sure museums will want them some day."

"No, Walter. I'm serious about this. My clients all have copies of their blueprints—they can give them to a museum if they want. I want all my papers destroyed before you leave tonight. Please promise me, Walter."

"Of course, Miss Morgan. I'd do anything you'd ask."

She smiled and seem relieved. She stood up from the desk, and picked up her shaw and umbrella. Walter Hake stood and faced her. He was surprised when she hugged him. In the thirty years they'd worked together, a few handshakes were the only physical contact they had ever shared.

"You take care of yourself, Walter."

"You too, ma'am. You too."

And with that, Julia Morgan left her office in the Merchants Exchange Building for the last time and returned to her house on Divisadero Street. For the next few years she only left that house a few times, and strongly discouraged guests from visiting her. She died there in her sleep one night six years later in the Winter of 1957.

Walter Hake stayed late on that last night of work,

destroying the records as Miss Morgan had requested. One of the last things left were her three leather-bound handwritten journals. She had written in these journals as long as he had known her.

He shook his head, and put the journals into a large envelope, and slipped it into his jacket. He had never refused a request of Miss Morgan's, but this was different. He just could not bring himself to destroy her journals—they needed to be preserved. And, besides, Miss Morgan would never know that he had not completely followed her wishes.

He carefully closed up the shop, and left the office to enjoy his life in retirement.

CHAPTER 4

San Francisco, California (Present Day)

Gabriel Patrick stumbled slightly as he got out of the back seat of the limousine. He looked around quickly, embarrassed that anyone might have witnessed his less than graceful exit from the car. The hotel bellman nodded slightly and smiled at him. Gabe gathered what dignity he could, and walked up the few red carpeted steps into the St. Francis hotel, as the bellman held the door open.

He entered the lobby and was suddenly aware of how bright it was compared to the darkness of the night. He glanced up at the gold plated baroque ceiling. It always surprised him how some things could be so simultaneously tacky, yet beautiful at the same time.

Even intoxicated, he was acutely aware of the history of the building around him. The St. Francis was one of the few buildings in San Francisco to survive the earthquake of 1906, only to burn a few hours later in the resulting firestorm. In the 1920s it had been the site of silent movie star Fatty Arbuckle's ill fated liaison with aspiring actress Virginia Rappe—which resulted in both the demise of the young girl and Fatty's career. Over fifty years later it had been the site of the attempted assassination of President Gerald Ford by Sara Jane Moore—one of Charles Manson's "girls."

Yes, these guided walls had been witness to a lot of history.

He was extremely aware of his steps as he walked through the lobby. He was trying very hard not to appear as if he had been drinking. But he feared it was a losing proposition.

He was pretty much a lightweight when it came to alcohol. Generally his limit was one glass of wine, or maybe a beer. Tonight, with one of the most expensive dinners he had probably ever eaten, he had consumed four glasses of a very rare vintage.

But, tonight had been a special night. He had recently completed an acquisition of a very rare piece of jewelry for a wealthy client, and the client had insisted on hosting a dinner at Fleur de Lys—a very upscale French restaurant in Nob Hill.

But, compared to the price that the client had paid

to acquire the necklace—and the price he paid to Gabe for finding it—the ten thousand dollar meal was a drop in the bucket. Of course, Lawrence Smithley was not just any client. At eighty-one years old, he was still one of the wealthiest, most powerful men in Northern California.

Smithley had contacted Gabe about six months earlier, having learned of his unique services through a business acquaintance. He was looking for a gold and emerald necklace that had originally belonged to his grandmother. It had been lost during the Great Quake of 1906, but had later been recovered in the 1920s after being found in the possessions of a now dead man who had stolen it during the cleanup. The necklace had then gone to his mother, and with her death he gave it to his own wife.

The necklace had been lost again, this time during the earthquake of 1989. As before, it had been stolen during the cleanup after the quake. Unlike the first time, however, instead of staying in the possession of the man who stole it, it changed hands several times in the less-than-reputable jewelry black market. After following its path over the years since its most recent disappearance, Gabe eventually tracked it down to a private dealer in Boston. At Lawrence Smithley's direction, he paid the dealer $250,000 to buy it back.

With Gabe's "finders fee" of $100,000 the old man had paid a fortune for a necklace that he technically already owned. And, he couldn't be happier.

That was really Gabe's favorite part of his business—the happiness that he could bring to people. And, of course, the money did not hurt. He only worked for a few clients a year, yet he was making more money than he ever had dreamed he could. Of course, as a former assistant professor of art history, his salary expectations had always been pretty low.

He started the business—which his former boyfriend Kevin had named "Lost Loves"—a few years ago. It was one of those situations that was just kismet. He had been fired from his faculty position at Ohio State (although, the polite term used was that his "contract was not renewed"), and he was floundering. He originally started the business as small gallery, but had been hired by a wealthy lady to find a specific set of antique dishes, and that experience began to redefine what his business would become.

Then, his former partner and professional mentor Rudolph Zeffner was murdered, and Kevin showed up in Columbus asking for his help. The personal situation between the three of them had been very complicated (and some would say—fairly sorted). The events which followed after that were so bizarre that even today, Gabe had a hard time believing himself that all of it had really happened. Those events had culminated in a show down with a cold-blooded killer on a dark lake on a moonless Autumn night.

Everything in Gabe's life seemed to fall into place after his experience that night on the lake. He and Kevin were once again very close friends, and he was the proud proprietor of a successful business that helped people reconnect with their own "lost loves." All in all, it was a pretty good life…

Gabe was startled from that pleasant thought by the sight of a familiar face on the TV in the lobby bar.

Jesus. What a way to ruin an evening, he thought.

The television was showing CNN and some footage recorded earlier in the day from a senate confirmation hearing on Capital Hill. He should not have been too surprised; he kept up with the news and he knew all about the President's nominee to be the new Secretary of the Interior. In fact, Gabe wished that he did not know nearly as much about him as he did.

Gabe turned away from the image. It had been a good day—he was not going to let that guy ruin it. Besides, he had been trying to be more forgiving lately—that whole idea about the kind of energy you put out into the universe is what you get back—or some similar Oprah platitude.

He was startled again by the ringing of his cell phone. He looked down at the caller ID display. It read *Molly Newman.*

Molly? She didn't know he was in California and it would have been a little after midnight by Columbus time. It was not like her to call this late.

He answered the phone on the second ring in a near panic.

"Molly—are Vickie and the baby ok?"

CHAPTER 5

Washington, DC (Present Day)

Reginald Allard took off his glasses and rubbed his eyes hard. He had been through a lot of tough situations in his career, but this was by far the hardest thing he had ever had to do.

He was sitting in a holding room in a back area of the United States Capital building. He felt like he had been waiting for hours, but when he looked at his watch he realized it had only been about twenty minutes. The smell of the leather furniture in the room seemed overpowering and somewhat nauseating.

He was waiting for his Senate hearing to begin with the Committee on Energy and Natural Resources. Once he survived this dog and pony show, his appointment would be put up for a vote by the whole Senate. It seemed like quite a production just to get the job of Secretary of the

Interior, and more stress than he wanted to experience. The bad part was this job was actually considered a "favor" by the administration for being such a good soldier for the Democratic party.

Last year he had made the decision not to run for a full term as Indiana's Governor. He would like to say that the decision was his alone, but the truth was he was strongly encouraged not to run by the party. In the months leading up to the announcement, he could not believe the number of prominent Democrats who had called him wanting to provide "advice" on his decision whether or not to run. Of course, the "advice" was all slanted one way—it seemed no one in the party wanted to see his name on the ballot in November. The final call he got was from the President's chief-of-staff, suggesting that if he would decide not to run, there could potentially be an opportunity for him in the administration.

That was pretty much all Reginald needed to hear. Of course, what no one realized is that he actually never intended to run. He was never supposed to be governor anyway—it was just a strange mistake of fate which made him the chief executive of Indiana to begin with.

He had been asked by Governor Kenneth "Butch" Waterton to run as his Lieutenant Governor in the previous election. Butch was running for his third term as governor, and was the rare breed of a popular Democrat in a red state. The governor had wanted to shake up his cabinet a little bit for this third go-around, and thought Reginald Allard would make a good number two.

Most political commentators thought it was an odd choice, since Allard had no previous experience as an elected official. His current job was president of Indiana University, and he had spent his entire career in academia. But after spending most of his life in Indiana politics, Butch Waterton had a pretty good sense of what would play well with his constituents. And, he was pretty sure Reginald Allard would play well.

During his tenure as president of IU, the school had won two back-to-back NCAA basketball championships, and had even finished second in the Big Ten in football one year. With every media mention of the school's athletic success, President Allard made sure his name—and the fact that he had personally recruited the new basketball and football coaches—was highlighted in every story. Butch Waterton wanted to bring a little of that public goodwill for college athletics into his campaign.

Like most of the governor's political instincts, this strategy played out just the way he thought that it would. He was reelected to a third term by a sizable margin over his Republican opponent—a rare feat in Indiana politics.

Reginald actually enjoyed being Lieutenant Governor. There was not a lot of responsibility associated with the role, and the job was a lot easier than being the president of a major university. He figured he could ride out this position through the governor's term, then maybe he could score a sweet deal on the corporate meeting lecture circuit.

But, then, the unthinkable happened. Two years into this third term, Butch Waterton suffered a massive coronary and died in the middle of a cabinet meeting. Reginald Allard was suddenly the accidental governor of Indiana.

In a split second, his entire life changed—and not for the better. While he enjoyed the trappings of the office, the work and responsibility were overwhelming. For a man who had spent his entire career in academia, he was completely over his head in this situation.

During the next few years, Reginald made every effort to just keep the status quo going and not make any major mistakes. In the background, the party machinery was working full steam to find a suitable candidate for the next election. They found that candidate in a young state senator from Fort Wayne.

So, he really had no qualms about stepping aside for someone else to pick up the heavy lifting—especially if it meant some sort of White House position for him. It had taken several months for the right opportunity to appear, but then the former Secretary of the Interior had resigned to accept a high paying job in the private sector.

He called the President's Chief-of-Staff, and in a veiled allusion to *quid pro quo*, he told the White House that Secretary of the Interior was the job he wanted. He believed it was perfect for him—after all, he held doctorates in both natural history and zoology. Plus, it was a cabinet level position, which Reginald very much wanted. After a few conversations with a few people high up in the administration (including a very brief call with the president himself), the president nominated him for the job.

That turn of events brought him to this waiting room in the capital this morning.

The door opened, and a pretty, young blonde woman stepped into the room. She smiled warmly.

"Governor, the committee is ready for you now."

Reginald Allard turned and followed her out the door.

CHAPTER 6

At first Molly was surprised by Gabe's reaction when he picked up the phone. She had never considered that by calling so late he would automatically assume something was wrong. And, based on their current situation, he would naturally assume there was something wrong with her partner Vickie or their soon to be born child.

"Oh, God Gabe—I'm sorry. I'm sorry to call so late, but I was on a plane. Everything is ok with Vickie and the baby."

Gabe let out a deep sigh. "Well, that's a relief. But it's actually not late for me either—I'm in San Francisco for work with a client."

"San Francisco? Seriously? I am too! In fact, that's what I'm calling you about. I was hoping you could dial in for a conference call, but if you're here that's even better!"

"You were calling me about San Francisco? What are you doing here?"

"Well, it's a long story," she said. "My brother Mark has gone missing, and I'm trying to track down some information that might help me find him."

"Mark is missing? What happened?"

"I'm not really sure. His girlfriend called me yesterday and said that it had been several days since she had heard from him and she was getting really worried."

"I didn't even know Mark had a girlfriend," Gabe replied.

"Yeah, me either. But Mark always did have a string of girls hanging around. I guess some women really get into the nerdy, moody type. But, for some reason, he's never had trouble attracting the ladies."

"A trait which runs in the Newman family, I guess."

Molly ignored the comment. They enjoyed the type of friendly ribbing that only people who have been close friends for a long time can. In many ways, Gabe felt more like a brother to her than Mark ever really did.

"Anyway," she continued, unwilling to give Gabe the satisfaction that she had even heard—let alone registered—the remark. "She said that Mark had told her that he would be gone for about a week on a trip to the Grand Canyon where he was doing research for his PhD dissertation. That was almost two weeks ago now, and she hasn't heard a word from him."

"I can see why she's worried. But, Molly, need I remind you that you're FBI? I'm not sure how I can help you beyond the resources you already have available."

"In this case, the bureau isn't really much of a help. In fact, I was told that the FBI did not have jurisdiction, and that this should be handled by the National Parks Service."

"The Parks Service? Do you even know for sure that he went to the Grand Canyon? Maybe he was just trying to let this girl down gently, and that seemed like a good story to tell her."

"I'd like to think my brother has a little more game going on than that… But, yes, I do know he was in the Grand Canyon. I was able to do a little digging through a friend in park administration, and they have a record of him registering at campground called Phantom Ranch four days ago. Also, he had been given a rafting permit for a single person craft access to the Colorado River that was valid from April first through the tenth."

Gabe looked at the calendar indicator on his watch. It was April 11th.

"Yeah, I can see why you are worried. But, I still don't understand how I can help?"

"I have a meeting scheduled tomorrow morning with

Mark's program advisor. I wanted you there to talk professor-to-professor."

"Molly, I'll do anything I can to help, but Mark is a cultural anthropologist—my specialization is in art history. I'm not sure how much help I'll be."

"Oh, don't sell yourself short," Molly said. "I'm sure you and Dr. Schmidt won't have any problem at all understanding each other. But, Gabe—I really want you there."

Gabe was surprised. Molly absolutely hated admitting to anyone that she needed help with anything. For her to say this, really made a statement about how concerned she actually was.

"Of course, Molly," Gabe said. "I'll be happy to go to the meeting with you. Where is it and what time should I be there?"

"It's at San Francisco State University at nine o'clock in the morning."

Gabe thought he could detect a note of relief in her voice.

"I had a key to Mark's place and I'm staying at his apartment in Lakeside tonight. What hotel are you staying in?"

"I'm at the St. Francis on Union Square."

"Ooooh—fancy. I guess the treasure hunting

business must be paying pretty well."

By the fact that she was now ribbing him, Gabe knew that this conversation must have made her feel better.

"Will you be taking the MUNI?" she asked.

"Yeah, that's probably the fastest considering what San Francisco traffic will be like during rush hour."

"Ok, great. I'll meet you at the station at SFSU at 8:45." She hesitated for a moment, then added "I really do appreciate you going with me."

"Of course, it's the least I could for the other expectant mother of my child, isn't it?"

Molly laughed.

"Yeah, ok. Get to bed and try to sleep it off. I don't want you to be hung over and make me late for that meeting tomorrow."

"How did you know I've had a few drinks?"

"I was a detective, remember? Plus, you're not exactly great at hiding it. From the amount of slurring on your words, I'd guess three glasses of wine."

"Four, actually," Gabe said, happy that he hadn't been quite as easy to read as she seemed to think.

"Wow. Must have been quite the party," she said, still laughing. "Just get some sleep, and I'll see you in the morning."

Gabe ended the call, and took the elevator to his

room on the eleventh floor. Through a combination of jet lag and the wine, he was sound asleep within fifteen minutes.

CHAPTER 7

Grand Canyon, Arizona (August 1882)

The Mexican man wiped his brow and looked up toward the nearly blinding sun. He had no idea of the temperature, but he knew it was extremely hot. He took out his canteen and took a big swig of water. He wanted more, but he knew he had to do his best to conserve. Running out of water out here would be a death sentence, and he doubted if his companion would share his water with him. If the situation was reversed, he was pretty sure he would not be willing to share his.

He and his companion had been out searching the desert for hours. He believed it to be a fool's folly to continue, but the boss man had insisted that they stay out and continue to search. The boss man refused to accept the reality of the situation—there was little hope that his ten-year-old daughter had not perished in the unforgiving desert.

The little girl had wandered away from the mining camp nearly two full days ago. It had been several hours before anyone even noticed that she was missing. By that point, she could have traveled miles in any direction. She had eaten dinner with her father and the other men in the camp, then had gone to her tent for the night. Her father had gone in to check on her before he went to bed and discovered she was missing.

Her father had taken several men and had gone out searching for her all night, with no sign of her anywhere. Since then, every waking minute of every man in the camp had been spent looking for the little girl. Earnesto Gonzalez understood why the man wanted to keep looking for his daughter, but he believed there was only one possibility at this point—young Julia Morgan must certainly be dead.

This canyon is a beautiful, but deadly place—no place for a child, Earnesto thought to himself.

He and his companion had been out searching for the little girl since daybreak. They had followed some marks that might have been footprints in a sandy bank along a smaller stream that fed off the Colorado River. Of course, they could have just as easily been the prints of a coyote or mountain lion, or possibly just the patterns of the wind in the sand. But, it gave them something to follow; some hope that they might be able to find some remnant of the little girl and give her poor father some peace.

Earnesto was ready to suggest that they turn around and head back toward camp, when something out of the corner of his eye caught his attention; a flash of red fluttering in the breeze several hundred feet up the canyon. He put his arm up to stop his companion from moving forward. He pointed up to the red figure high on the ledge above them.

His companion took out a small pair of binoculars and trained them on the area where Earnesto pointed.

"It looks...it looks like a person," he said in Spanish.

Earnesto nodded. He was afraid that might be the case.

The two men looked around and saw that there was a crude trail leading up toward the cliff where they saw the figure. They began the slow climb up the trail in the stifling heat.

About five hundred feet above the canyon floor, they came upon a wide flat ledge that ended into an opening in the cliff face. Laying in front of the cave opening, about twenty feet from them was the figure in red—it was a small child. It was little Julia Morgan.

Earnesto swallowed hard, and started to walk slower as they approached the body of the little girl. He was not prepared for what the poor child must look like after being out in the elements. He dreaded having to take her back to her father; no parent should have to see their child like that.

However, as he got closer he realized there was something odd about the scene. What struck him as odd was not what he saw, but what he did not see. There were no vultures. With a dead body laying out in the open like this, the vultures should have completely picked it clean by now.

Then, he saw something even more surprising. The body was moving. Earnesto and his companion began running toward the child.

Earnesto fell to his knees and turned the little girl's face toward him.

"Señorita Morgan?" he said softly.

She opened her eyes and smiled at him.

He pulled out his canteen, and poured a little of the water into the girl's mouth. She started to choke, and he helped her sit up.

"Señorita Morgan, how did you get here?"

But the girl was obviously too weak to speak. She was wearing a long decorated red gown that looked like it was made of silk. Earnesto was positive she had not been wearing such a garment earlier; she had been dressed in clothing far more appropriate for the mining camp. He reached down and pulled her up toward his chest. He noticed she was clutching an object in her hand; it looked like a small, gold broach.

Then, something else grabbed Earnesto's attention.

From within the cave he could hear sounds. At first they were very faint, but they were getting increasingly louder. Earnesto was sure he was hearing voices coming from deep within the cave. The voices seemed to be synchronized, almost like some sort of religious chant.

He looked at his companion, almost hoping he was imagining this. His companion did not turn to look at Earnesto; instead he was staring wide-eyed and open mouthed into the cave. Earnesto knew the other man was hearing it too.

"*A Dios mio,*" the man said while making the sign of the cross.

Both men had heard the stories of the underground dwellers that the Indians told. The Hopis called them the *Hisatinom*, or "the people of long ago." The Navajo referred to them as the *Anasazi*—"the ancient enemies." Until today, Earnesto had always just considered them myths of a superstitious people. Today, he was no longer so sure.

Earnesto snapped to attention, shaking off the almost hypnotic tone of the chants. He stood up and picked up the little girl in one smooth motion. Then he and his companion began the long trek back down the steep path.

Charles Morgan was absolutely beside himself with joy when his young daughter was returned to him. He gave Earnesto and his companion $50 each, which was practically a fortune to the two men.

Morgan left the mining camp with his daughter to seek medical assistance in Flagstaff. The doctor gave young Julia a clean bill of health, and seemed disbelieving that this child could have actually spent two days lost in the desert. She demonstrated none of the health issues that would surely result from such an ordeal.

Morgan decided to cut the rest of his mining exploration short and return to San Francisco. He had suggested to his daughter that they may not want to mention the events of those days to her mother. Julia readily agreed— she knew her mother's reaction would be to never let her accompany her father on one of these trips again, and she desperately did not want that to happen.

There was very little Julia would have been able to tell her mother anyway. She remembered very little of the entire event. She could recall hearing voices from her tent on the night she had disappeared. She had gone outside the tent to investigate the sounds. The next thing she knew, she was waking up on a ledge high about the canyon floor, staring into the face of a Mexican man who looked as though he had just seen a ghost.

She could remember nothing of those lost few days. That was true, at least, when she was awake.

In her dreams was another story. In her dreams she could recall the adventure in vivid detail, and her extensive conversations with the ancient ones. She never actually spoke with them in the traditional sense, but rather, she would hear their voices in her mind.

You are a special child, they would say. *You are destined to do wonderful things; it is your fate. We sought you out to teach you of our ways and our civilization. It was the prophecy that you would come to us, and someday you would protect us. We give you this amulet to remember us and with it the information needed to return to us someday.*

In the beginning, she would wake up with only the fuzziest recollection of her dreams. As she grew older, the memories became more concrete, but never completely clear. Her understanding of those people eventually developed into some sort of sixth sense, as opposed to factual understanding.

While always a bright child, her intellect soared after the lost days in the desert. She was filled with curiosity on every conceivable topic and subject. Her artistic ability flourished. It almost felt to her like she was a different person, but the changes seemed invisible to all those around her.

She would write for hours in her journals; exploring her understanding of the messages, and speculating on their meaning. She always kept the amulet close by her, but kept it hidden from view. Her father had known that she had it when she was returned to the mining camp, but he completely forgot about it afterward. He had no idea that she carried it with her at all times; or at least until she had to sacrifice it many years later to protect the ancient ones—just as they had told her.

CHAPTER 8

Washington, DC (Current Day)

Yes, senator—of course I'm a strong advocate of species protection and maintaining the integrity of the sanctuary. However, I also understand that controlled hunting is actually often the best course of protection for a population," he paused for a moment, then looked toward the Republican senator from Wyoming. "And, being born and raised in the midwest, I recognize the cultural importance of hunting as well."

Reginald Allard sat back against his chair, pleased with his answer. He had been coached quite extensively by the White House to help prepare him for the hearing. It had obviously been a good use of his time, since he believed he had just given a near perfect answer to the Senator from Virginia's question about controlled hunting seasons. His response had a little something for everyone—the tree huggers and the red necks.

He fought the urge to smile; it would not be good to appear too smug when testifying before a congressional committee.

The questions from the senators continued for the next ninety minutes. Most of the questions posed to him would be considered softball at best. He noticed that by about an hour in, several of the cable news networks had packed up their cameras and left. There would be no great political theater in this hearing room today.

The White House had prepared him that the hearing may last a few days, based on their most recent experiences with confirmations. However, it was pretty clear to Allard that this phase would probably be wrapped up by the end of today at the latest.

I guess he should not have been too surprised; this congress and the President had a lot more important battles facing them than just the confirmation of some low-level secretary. As much as he usually enjoyed the spotlight and being known as a rabble rouser, in this situation Reginald Allard was happy to be flying under the radar.

As his question about hunting indicated, he brought a little something for everyone. He was a lifelong Democrat, which fit well with the administration and the current makeup of the Senate. But, he had also been the chief executive of a red state, and had been a pro-business governor, so the Republicans did not have much of an issue with him either. He was practically the textbook definition of a moderate centrist.

And, as much as it might normally hurt his ego, Reginald Allard realized that he was simply a non-issue. This time, that suited him just fine.

After the hearing was completed he was led back to the same leather upholstered waiting room where he had spent the morning. He had no idea how long the committee's debate and subsequent vote would take, but he felt good about his performance.

He sat down in one of the large leather chairs and begin to browse through the day's edition of the Washington Post. He was barely into the second section of the paper when the pretty blonde woman from the morning interrupted him.

The committee had completed their vote, and he had been unanimously recommended to have his appointment put before the full Senate for the confirmation vote.

Reginald Allard finally allowed himself to smile. If all went well, he would be sworn in as the next Secretary of the Interior by the end of the week.

CHAPTER 9

San Francisco, California (Present Day)

Gabe had left the St. Francis around 8:00 in the morning, and made the short walk down Powell Street to the intersection of Market. The bright morning sun felt good on his face. Despite the overindulgence in wine the previous evening, he felt surprisingly good today.

It was early in the morning, yet the corner was already crowded with tourists at the terminus of the cable car route. Gabe turned sharply to the right to avoid the crowd, and headed down the stairs to the Powell and Market MUNI station. From here he would take a green line train to the stop at San Francisco State University.

He was surprised that the train was not completely packed considering it was technically still rush hour. He found a seat toward the middle of one of the trains where he could see the system map posted on the wall of the car.

He had originally planned on flying back to Columbus today, but after the call from Molly last night he had logged on to the airline's web site early this morning to change his travel plans. His main priority now was to help Molly.

He had only known Molly for a few years, but they had grown amazingly close during that time. He met her shortly after he started his gallery and had joined the Olde Towne East community association. Molly had been the Columbus Police Department liaison to the group.

They had hit it off almost immediately, which was rare for Gabe—it normally took him a while to feel comfortable with people. But for what ever reason, he felt that he had found a kindred spirit in Molly Newman, and she felt the same way.

At the time, Molly lived only a few blocks from Gabe with her partner Vickie. Molly and Vickie had been together for over twenty years, having met each other as college freshman at Bowling Green. While Gabe always liked to tease her about how lesbians could go straight from the first date to picking out china, he really admired (and was a little envious of) what Molly and Vickie had together. Maybe he would find the same thing himself someday.

Molly had literally saved Gabe and Kevin's life during

the firefight with Rudy's killer by teaming up with the FBI and intervening to save them. These events only served to bring Gabe and Molly closer together, although it also resulted in her coming up with a new favorite nickname for Gabe—"treasure hunting flamer." Gabe wasn't really wild about the title, but he would let her have her fun. After all, he had teasingly referred to her as much worse many times. That was the kind of relationship they had, and why Gabe wondered many times if they had been siblings in some former life.

Shortly after the adventure which resulted in Gabe's nickname, Molly was accepted into the FBI academy. It was her career dream come true, and Gabe was happy that he had played some small role in that. Even if that role consisted of almost getting himself and his ex-boyfriend killed.

Molly spent twenty two weeks at the FBI Academy in Quantico, and graduated with honors. She was now on her first field assignment at the FBI field office in Phoenix, Arizona.

About a year ago, when Molly was home in Columbus from a break at the academy, she had told Gabe that she wanted to go out for a drink—just the two of them. Molly seemed odd to Gabe that night; she seemed nervous and jumpy—not at all her normal self. Finally, he asked her what was wrong. She told him that she and Vickie had been talking a lot about having a baby, and they would really like for Gabe to be the donor and biological father of their child.

Gabe was absolutely thrilled, and had agreed to it nearly before Molly had a chance to get the whole sentence out. He had always dreamed of being a father himself, and while he would not actually be a parent to this child, he loved the idea of being part of bringing a baby into the world, and doing this favor for his two close friends.

A few trips to a fertility specialist at Ohio State later, and Vickie was pregnant. The baby was due to be born in only a few weeks now. Gabe was already planning to make the trip to Phoenix when he was born. (Molly had refused to be told the gender of the baby before it was born; Gabe and Vickie on the other hand could not wait to find out, and was finding it hard now to avoid masculine pronouns around Molly.)

Once outside of the inner city, the MUNI train rose from underground, and paralleled U.S. Route 1 as it headed out toward the suburbs. Gabe had not spent much time in this part of the city, and was surprised at how residential it appeared compared to the touristy areas of San Francisco he normally frequented.

The train rolled into the San Francisco State University station, and Gabe exited the MUNI. He got off the train and saw Molly standing across the street waiting for him, holding two cups of steaming coffee. Once again he was reminded of why he liked her so much.

"Hey, stranger," he said walking up to her and smiling. "You look right at home standing on the street corner."

"I've learned it from the best," she said, returning the smile. "I thought you might need some coffee—I imagine you're feeling a little rough this morning."

"Actually, I feel great. Maybe wine that costs more than my first car really agrees with me."

Gabe took his coffee cup from Molly, and they began walking into the university campus.

"We're meeting with Dr. Abigail Schmidt. She is Mark's program advisor, and I'm hoping she can give us some information about why he would be in the Grand Canyon and where he was heading."

"So, being an FBI agent hasn't been a real advantage in this situation, huh?"

"Not at all actually—other than me having a contact in park administration. Mark isn't even technically missing according to the authorities—it's been less than a week since anyone has heard from him, and extended trips by rafters and hikers in the canyon is not at all uncommon."

Gabe nodded in understanding.

"Of course," Molly said. "I don't think my asshole

partner helps the cause at all either. I think I could have talked my field office supervisor into at least letting me take a look at the case, if he wouldn't have been so against it."

"So, you've gone rogue, huh?" Gabe asked, still smiling.

"I had some personal days coming to me. If I decide to use them investigating my missing brother, that's my business."

"So, what's the deal with your partner? Sounds like you're not a big fan."

"He's a pretty-boy, boy scout, by-the-book uptight closet case," she hesitated for a moment, then added. "On second thought, I'm sure you two would get along great." Molly gave Gabe a wide smile with the last sentence.

Gabe was happy to see that despite her worry over her brother, Molly had not lost her biting sense of humor.

"So, you don't have any idea why he was going to the Grand Canyon?"

"Not really. I'm sure it had something to do with his doctoral dissertation and some theory he was working on. He was always talking about it, but you know how those academic things bore me."

Gabe knew exactly what she meant. On more than one occasion, Gabe had tried to engage Molly in some sort of philosophical or academic conversation, and she would always show absolutely no interest. She was more focused on the realities of the here and now, not some theoretical rhetoric. He supposed that is what made her such a good cop.

"I spent last night at Mark's apartment not too far from here—luckily, he had given me a spare key."

"Find anything interesting," Gabe asked.

"Nada. My brother's life appears to be more boring than I ever imagined—he doesn't even have cable!"

"Yeah, believe it or not, some people don't spend all their free time with the Kardashians."

"Well, those people miss out on a lot. Let's pick up the pace, I don't want to be late for our meeting with Dr. Schmidt."

Gabe and Molly negotiated their way across the main lawn of the campus, avoiding the throngs of students rushing to their morning classes.

CHAPTER 10

San Francisco State University

D r. Abigail Schmidt looked up at her office wall clock. It was five minutes before nine o'clock and she was expecting her morning appointment to arrive at any moment.

She was simultaneously nervous, worried, and feeling guilty.

She was nervous because she was not in the habit of having meetings with the FBI. Even though the woman assured her this was not an official visit; she was Mark Newman's sister and she was hoping to gain some insight on what could have happened to him.

She was worried because she genuinely cared about the young man, and she was concerned about what fate might have befallen him. She had expected to hear from him by now as well, but had told herself that the expedition was just taking longer than expected. However, since the call from Mark's sister yesterday she had grown very concerned.

She was feeling guilty because she believed she should have done more to dissuade Mark from his dissertation subject. No, it was not the subject that was the problem—it was how he planned to pursue it. She had told him that it was a dangerous expedition, and more than likely would turn out to be a wild goose chase. After all, the stories of the Egyptian treasure in the Grand Canyon had been around for a century, and no one yet had ever found any trace of its existence. What's more, no one had ever been able to prove that any of the individuals mentioned in the 1909 newspaper story ever even existed!

Yes, she should have done more to talk him out of it…

She tried to shake the feelings, but it was difficult. Abigail had spent a large part of her life feeling guilty about one thing or another.

She had been born in England nearly sixty years ago to parents who were strawberry farmers. Her father had been captured as a German prisoner of war and taken to an English POW camp when he was just a teenager. With all of his family in Germany dead, he became somewhat of a surrogate child to the old couple who owned the strawberry farm where he had been assigned to work. They asked him to stay on with them after the war, and the couple (who had no children of their own) left the farm to her father in their will.

Abigail had come to the United States to go to college, and had lived here ever since. After her mother died of cancer during graduate school she felt guilty about being so far away from her family, but she was busy with her studies. She told herself she would spend more time with her father after she had graduated. But, then, she started work on her doctorate and got married (albeit very briefly), and always had difficulty finding the time.

In the Summer of 2005 her father died, and she realized she had only seen him five times in the twenty-plus years since her mother had died. They talked on the phone weekly, but it just wasn't the same.

She felt horrible that she had always chosen work and the convenience of her life instead of making the time for him. She hated that she had never insisted that he come to visit her in California; she knew he would have loved San Francisco. But most of all, she hated that she carried all of these regrets.

Her father had died of a suspected heart attack while sitting on the front porch of the farmhouse. One of the neighborhood children had seen him laying on the porch from the road, and had alerted the local police. It hurt her deeply to think that he had died alone.

Although, there one thing that she had always confused her about the situation of his death. The police reported there being two tea cups on the porch table; one was her father's (which apparently shattered when he was felled by the attack), but one was full and sitting on the side table between the two porch chairs.

She had always wondered who the other cup of tea had been for…

Her thoughts were interrupted by a woman and a man standing in the doorway to her office.

"Dr. Schmidt? I'm Molly Newman—I called yesterday about meeting with you this morning?"

Abigail rose from behind her desk and walked toward her visitors, her right hand extended.

"Of course, of course, Agent Newman," she said with a warm smile, and shaking both their hands. "Please come in."

Abigail sat down at a small round conference table in the corner of her office, and motioned for Molly and Gabe to sit as well.

"This is my good friend, Gabe Patrick," Molly said. "I asked him to come with me today because I thought he would better understand the research that Mark was doing."

"Oh, are you an anthropologist as well, Mr. Patrick?"

"Art history actually," he said. "I was on faculty at

Ohio State, and now run somewhat of an art consulting business for collectors."

"Well, one certainly can't understand a society's culture without understanding its art. The two are always intertwined, aren't they?"

"I've always believed so, yes."

"Dr. Schmidt," Molly said, her impatience beginning to show. "I'll get right to the point. My brother has been missing for several days and I'm very worried"

Abigail nodded, her hospitable smile clouding to a look of concern.

"I've been able to confirm through the Park Service that Mark was kayaking in the the Grand Canyon, and that he was least seen at a campground on the canyon floor near something called Phantom Ranch."

Abigail nodded again, not wanting to interrupt the FBI agent's train of thought.

"Unfortunately, the canyon is a huge place, and without some sort of idea of where he was going or what he was looking for, we have absolutely no idea where to even begin to search for him. That's what we were hoping you could tell us—why was Mark in the Grand Canyon?"

Abigail Schmidt sat back in her chair and looked at the younger woman questioning her. The agent's concern was palpable—and contagious.

"Agent Newman—"

"Please call me Molly."

"Molly, I'm very worried about Mark as well. I had a lot of qualms about his plans for this expedition, but he was quite insistent on pursuing this course."

"You don't need to tell me how bull headed my brother can be, Dr. Schmidt. Once he sets his mind on something its nearly impossible to change it."

That must be something that runs in the family, Gabe thought to himself.

"Are you familiar with the theory of Diffusionism?" Abigail asked.

Molly looked at Gabe.

"Somewhat," Gabe said. "I believe its the theory that all cultures have influenced all other cultures—that the entire history of civilization is an ongoing continuum."

"Exactly. It completely discards the silo approach to understanding civilizations that the accepted history texts have always taught."

"And Mark's disappearance has something to do with this diffusionism theory?" Molly asked.

"I believe he went missing while he was attempting to prove the theories of Dr. Grafton Elliot Smith."

Both Molly and Gabe looked at her with no recognition of the name, so Abigail continued her explanation.

"Dr. Smith was an Australian medical doctor who specialized in human brain research. His interest in the physicality of the brain led to an interest in how human civilizations developed. He spent most of his career in England and Egypt—he had catalogued the human brain collection at the British Museum, and had been chair of anatomy at the Cairo School of Medicine."

Molly had to consciously stop herself from rolling her hand in a *hurry up* motion. She knew that Dr. Schmidt was trying to help them understand, but she wasn't getting to the bottom line as quickly as Molly would like. It was like when she would ask Gabe a simple question, then have to endure some five minute historical lecture before he would get to the point. But then again, Vickie was always telling her that she was far too impatient. So instead, Molly just nodded at Dr. Schmidt, urging her to continue.

"Dr. Smith actually formulated the theory of *hyperdiffusionism*."

Again, Gabe and Molly looked at her with no signs of recognition of the term.

"Hyperdiffusionism is that idea that not only have all cultures throughout history been influenced by one another, but all civilization actually sprung from one ancient, master civilization. Smith believed that master civilization originated in Egypt."

"How could that be?" Gabe asked. "We have archeological proof of civilizations older than the Egyptians—the Mesopotamians, the Sumerians, even some sites in China."

"Smith believed that there was a thriving culture in the Nile valley even before those, existing thousands of years before PreDynastic Egypt."

Gabe considered what she said, but looked somewhat skeptical.

"Smith believed that these very early Egyptians spread their culture around the world, long before any of the so-called ancient civilizations you mentioned came to be. He believed he had found evidence of this lost Egyptian culture all around the planet—even in such remote places as Polynesia."

"Ok," Molly said, losing the final bit of patience she was struggling to maintain. "That's all really interesting, but it still doesn't tell me why Mark was in the Grand Canyon."

Abigail stood up from her chair at the table and walked across her office to a large filing cabinet. She opened one of the drawers, and fished around it until she pulled out a document encased in a clear plastic protective cover. She handed the item to Molly, who shared it with Gabe.

It was a reprint of a newspaper article from the

Phoenix Gazette, and dated April, 1909. Gabe read the headline:

EXPLORATIONS IN GRAND CANYON
Mysteries of Immense Rich Cavern being brought to light;
Jordan is enthused; Remarkable finds indicate ancient people
migrated from Orient

"This article ran in an Arizona newspaper in 1909. It tells the story of an accidental discovery of Egyptian treasure in a cave in the Grand Canyon, and a plan by the Smithsonian to launch an expedition of the site," Dr. Schmidt said.

"I've never heard anything about this before," Gabe said. "I don't recall anything about a Smithsonian expedition in the Grand Canyon like this."

"That's because, from all information available—it never occurred."

Gabe and Molly looked at her quizzically.

"In fact, if you contact the Smithsonian," the anthropologist looked at Molly, then added. "As your brother did—they will tell you that they have no records of any such planned expedition. What's more, they have no record that Professor S.A. Jordan who was listed in the article as the spokesperson for the institution ever even existed—let alone worked for the Smithsonian."

Abigail Schmidt paused for a moment to measure whether her visitors seemed to grasp what she was saying. They did.

"What's more," she continued. "There's no record of the fellow who was credited with the original find—G.E. Kincaid. If it wasn't for the newspaper story, there would be absolutely no record that the discovery occurred."

"Did the discovery occur?" Molly asked. "This wouldn't be the only time that a hoax article appeared in a newspaper—take Roswell, for instance."

Gabe rolled his eyes. He and Molly had more heated discussions over the 1948 events in Roswell, New Mexico than probably anything else they enjoyed arguing about. Molly tended to believe the U.S. Government's official account. Gabe, however, tended to lean more toward the conspiracy theories.

"I have no idea whether the discovery actually occurred or not," Dr. Schmidt said. "But your brother was convinced of its authenticity. He was very excited about some recent discoveries he had made in the research of the topic."

"What were those discoveries?" Gabe asked.

"I don't know—he said he needed to complete some additional study first before he could fill me in on the details. But he told me he needed some time away from the university to pursue his ideas. I knew part of that involved the investigation at the Grand Canyon, but I got the distinct feeling there were other locations involved in his research."

"And, you didn't find that unusual?" Molly asked.

"No, not really. I have a great amount of professional respect for your brother, agent—," Abigail paused for a moment. "—Molly. I thought he needed the freedom to conduct the project the way he felt most comfortable. He could be a secretive and guarded person, but I respected his approach."

Once again, Gabe thought the anthropologist could have been just as easily describing Molly as her brother. Apparently, the figurative apples had not fallen far from this particular family tree.

"I realize that this whole thing must sound crazy," Dr. Schmidt said. "But I can tell you that after studying the history of human cultures for my entire career, there's a lot more we don't understand than we actually do. The history of human kind is a long tale, full of contradictions and mystery."

Both visitors looked somewhat disappointed and dejected.

Once again, Abigail Schmidt felt guilty. This time because this nice woman had come to her seeking help with finding her missing brother, and she hadn't really been able to give her anything concrete to work with.

Then, a thought occurred to her.

"Would you like to take a look around Mark's office and files to see if you can find any information that would be helpful? Normally I would disapprove of such an invasion of privacy, but in this case…"

For the first time since starting this meeting, Molly felt herself smile. Now she was going to get a chance to do her type of research.

CHAPTER 11

San Francisco State University

Mark's office was located on the lower level of the Anthropology building in a cramped space he shared with another PhD candidate. Gabe was somewhat pleased to see that the tradition of putting graduate students into less than desirable office space had not changed since his days at Ohio State.

Mark's office mate was doing a research project in Kenya, and had been out of the country for the entire semester. From the thin coating of dust which covered most surfaces in the office, Gabe imagined it had been quite a while since the office had been used by either of its occupants.

"Doesn't look like anyone has been here too recently," Molly said. She obviously had reached the same conclusion as Gabe.

The office was stuffy and uncomfortably warm. There was only one window in the room, high along the wall near the intersection with the ceiling. Molly pulled over a side chair to the window, climbed upon it and pushed the basement window hard. It opened, and a cool breeze greeted them. The sounds of a busy college campus wafted in from outside.

Molly found Mark's desk, indicated by his desktop nameplate. She noticed that there was only one framed picture on his desk. It was a picture of Molly and Mark laying in a hammock hanging between two palm trees. Molly recognized the photo; it had been taken when she was nine and Mark was four, and they were living in Pensacola where her father was stationed for a few years. She remembered it as being a very simple and happy time in her life. It touched her that Mark obviously remembered it that way too.

She began to look through a stack of papers on Mark's desk and found another copy of the *Phoenix Gazette* article that Dr. Schmidt had shown them. Whereas Dr. Schmidt's version had been a hard copy printout from a microfiche reader, Mark had obviously printed his copy from the Internet. Molly handed the article to Gabe.

Gabe began reading through the article on the treasure found in the Grand Canyon by one Mr. G.E. Kincaid. He noticed that Mark had highlighted several sections in the article. He read the first bright yellow passage.

> *According to the story related to the Gazette by Mr.*
> *Kincaid, the archaeologists of the Smithsonian Institute, which*
> *is financing the expeditions, have made discoveries which*
> *almost conclusively prove that the race which inhabited this*
> *mysterious cavern, hewn in solid rock by human hands, was*
> *of oriental origin, possibly from Egypt, tracing back to Ramses.*
> *If their theories are borne out by the translation of the tablets*
> *engraved with hieroglyphics, the mystery of the prehistoric*
> *peoples of North America, their ancient arts, who they were*
> *and whence they came, will be solved. Egypt and the Nile, and*
> *Arizona and the Colorado will be linked by a historical chain*
> *running back to ages which staggers the wildest fancy of the*
> *fictionist.*

Gabe read a little further, and found the next section
that Mark had highlighted. This contained a direct quote
from G.E. Kincaid about the location of the mystery cave.

> *First, I would impress that the cavern is nearly*
> *inaccessible. The entrance is 1,486 feet down the sheer canyon*
> *wall. It is located on government land and no visitor will be*
> *allowed there under penalty of trespass. The scientists wish*
> *to work unmolested, without fear of archeological discoveries*
> *being disturbed by curio or relic hunters. A trip there would be*
> *fruitless, and the visitor would be sent on his way.*

"Sounds like old G.E. wanted to discourage anyone from trying to go after his treasure," Gabe said, but Molly was too distracted trying to log into Mark's computer to acknowledge the observation.

Gabe continued skimming the article until the next highlighted portion.

Over a hundred feet from the entrance is the cross-hall, several hundred feet long, in which are found the idol, or image, of the people's god, sitting cross-legged, with a lotus flower or lily in each hand. The cast of the face is oriental, and the carving is similar. The idol almost resembles Buddha, though the scientists are not certain as to what religious worship it represents. Taking into consideration everything found thus far, it is possible that this worship most resembles the ancient people of Tibet.

"From the description in the article, he claimed to have found artifacts that were a mix of Egyptian and Asian in origin," Gabe said. This time, Molly stopped working at the computer and acknowledged the remark.

"That doesn't make any sense, does it?"

"Well, not from the traditionalist view of history. But if you subscribe to the theory of cultural diffusionism like your brother, it could provide some compelling evidence that your theory is correct."

Gabe continued through the article. The last section Mark had not only highlighted, but marked with a star in red marker.

Upwards of 50,000 people could have lived in the caverns comfortably. One theory is that the present Indian tribes found in Arizona are descendants of the serfs or slaves of the people which inhabited the cave. Undoubtedly a good many thousands of years before the Christian era, a people lived here which reached a high stage of civilization. The chronology of human history is full of gaps.

"If this article is accurate, this cavern is absolutely huge."

Again, Molly ignored him.

"Finally!"

Gabe looked over to what she was doing at the desk. She had successfully logged into Mark's computer.

"How did you know his password?" he asked.

"Luckily, my brother is pretty predictable. We had three dogs growing up—all of them were named Rambo. The second one was his favorite—so I tried rambo2 as the password. That was it."

Gabe walked behind Molly and looked over her shoulder at the computer screen. He pointed to an area of the computer desktop.

"It looks like he uses a cloud-based note keeping application," Gabe explained. "I use the same one—you can access your notes from your computer or from your phone."

Molly double-clicked the program's icon, and the online notes application opened. She double-clicked a notebook titled *THE Project*.

The first document contained dozens of images of variations of the swastika symbol. She looked back over her shoulder at Gabe, obviously confused by what she was seeing.

"Why would he have all this Nazi shit?"

"It's not Nazi shit," Gabe said. "They are variations of a swastika."

"Yeah, I know—Nazi shit."

"Actually," Gabe said. "Based on the long history of the symbol, that's only a very recent connection. It's only been in the 20th Century that people began to consider the swastika a symbol of evil."

Molly sighed and sat back against the chair. He was in full professor mode now, and she knew it was pointless to stop him until he was finished. Gabe continued the explanation.

"The swastika is actually one of the oldest symbols in

human history—it's been found on items over three thousand years old. Prior to the 20th century, it was always considered a symbol of good energy and good luck. Some U.S. soldiers in the First World War even wore the swastika on their uniform for good luck. Swastika actually derives from a Sanskrit word which means *lucky object*. I used to do a whole section on the swastika in a course I used to teach on artistic symbolism."

He could tell that Molly seemed less than interested on the origin of his knowledge on this subject.

"Ok," she said. "Why would Mark care so much about swastikas, and what would it have to do with his research?'

"Well, the symbol has been found in nearly every culture on Earth from Egypt, to China, to India—even in early Native American sites."

"So, cultural diffusionism would be the explanation for that?"

"Yes," Gabe said. "That's certainly one popular theory. Of course, there are competing theories that say that by the very nature of the simple shape of the swastika, it would develop organically and independently in any basket weaving culture."

He looked at Molly who was staring at him. She was obviously waiting for him to make a point.

"However," he finally said. "I'd be willing to bet

Mark's interest in the swastika were related to his research on diffusionism."

"But, still—it doesn't get us any closer to finding Mark."

Gabe nodded in agreement. As interesting as he thought this subject was, she was exactly right.

Molly opened another document in the online note taking program which had no title. She read the three entries.

Trevor Hake 805-555-7436
Freer 16 gal
B Honantewa

"Does any of that make any sense to you?"

"No," Gabe said. "Except of course that first one looks like a name and phone number."

Molly nodded, and she wrote down all three lines. She opened another document; this one contained multiple photos of an Egyptian-looking statue in a garden setting. Again, she looked to Gabe for explanation.

"It's a Sekhmet," Gabe said. "An Egyptian goddess with the body of a woman and the head of a lioness. She was the warrior goddess, and the daughter of the Sun God Ra. The Egyptians referred to her as the one before whom evil trembles."

"She sounds like my kind of woman," Molly said. "Any idea where this statue might be located?"

"No, I'm sorry. She's a pretty common symbol in Egyptian mythology, and there's not really enough in the setting of those photos to get a good idea of location."

Molly nodded, and pulled out her cell phone and began to dial.

"Who are you calling?"

"Trevor Hake."

Molly pushed the speaker phone button on her iPhone. The phone rang several times before a friendly young woman answered.

"Thanks for calling the Hearst San Simeon State Historical Monument, this is Mary how can I help you?"

Molly looked at Gabe, raising her eyebrow in surprise. Gabe shrugged his shoulders in return. *The Hearst Castle?*

"Hi Mary, I'm trying to reach Trevor Hake—I was wondering if he might be available?"

"One moment ma'am," the young woman said.

The next thing Molly heard was an on hold message giving tourist information about visiting the state historical monument. A few moments later, Mary returned to the line.

"No ma'am I'm sorry, Trevor is not working today. He's scheduled to be at work tomorrow morning."

Molly thanked the woman and hung up her phone.

"So, what now?" Gabe asked.

"I guess I'm heading to San Simeon. Trevor Hake is currently the only lead I have right now in finding Mark. I need to go ask him why my brother had his name and phone number."

"Mind if I tag along for the ride?"

Molly smiled widely.

"I was hoping you would."

CHAPTER 12

San Simeon, California (Present Day)

Gabe never realized that eight hours in a car could seem so long.

After leaving the university, He and Molly returned to the St. Francis so that he could retrieve his luggage from the hotel. Then, they found an Avis office on Post Street near Union Square so that they could rent a car for the drive down to San Simeon. It was shortly after Noon when they headed South out of San Francisco on the Pacific Coast Highway.

Normally, taking Highway 101 South then cutting over toward the coast at San Simeon would have been the faster route. However, the traffic alert in the rental car's GPS unit was reporting a major accident near Salinas that had traffic tied up for hours. Based on that information, taking the PCH all the way down to San Simeon seemed the more timely option.

The first few hours of the drive were very pleasant; Gabe throughly enjoyed the vast views of the Pacific on his right, and the mountains rising to the left. Molly was pretty quiet during most of the trip, but he was sure it was because she was worried about Mark. That was OK—that gave him time to think and enjoy the ride. That was, until they got to the other side of Monterey.

They passed through Monterey right around dusk, and south of the city the landscape of the PCH changed pretty dramatically. The smooth wide lanes with beach on one side, and farm fields on the other, changed into a cliff-hugging drive hanging over the sea. It was getting dark, and the hairpin turns of the narrow road had Gabe on edge.

It did not seem to bother Molly at all, and Gabe noted that her driving speed did not seem to be decreasing to reflect his perception of the current road conditions.

"Hey, Danica Patrick," he said, trying not sound as nervous as he felt. "I'm not ready to do a Princess Grace over one of these cliffs."

Molly rolled her eyes at the comment.

"I'm driving the speed limit—more or less."

"Yeah, it's the 'more' part that is concerning me."

Molly continued to drive on, and as the night got darker, the PCH got even more perilous as it headed down the coast toward Big Sur. As the turns got sharper, Gabe found himself getting more and more carsick with each passing mile.

"Molly," he finally said out of desperation, "I really think I'm going to puke if we don't stop for a minute."

Molly pulled the car over to a small area to the right. A sign proclaimed it to be a scenic outlook, but it was really little more than just a wide spot on the side of the road. It was too dark to see what made the view so scenic, but Gabe could hear the ocean crashing on the rocks a few hundred feet below them.

Molly was trying to be patient, but she was in a hurry to get down to San Simeon so that they could confront Trevor Hake first thing in the morning. She looked at her watch several times, as Gabe felt his nausea slowly subside.

"Are you about ready to get on the road again?" She asked, when her patience had finally reached its end.

"Ok, but how about I drive for a while?"

Molly handed Gabe the car keys, and walked around to the passenger door.

This arrangement only lasted about fifteen minutes.

"Jesus, Gabe—you drive like my grandmother!"

Within a few minutes, they had stopped again, and once again traded places. This pattern repeated itself a few more times until they finally reached an area of safer road

South of Ragged Point.

They pulled into the outskirts of San Simeon shortly after Midnight. Once again, the PCH had opened into a wide four-lane highway. Gabe felt immediately more comfortable.

"Any preference on a hotel for the night?" Gabe asked.

Molly looked to the right side of the road and a Motel 6 with a flashing light proclaiming Vacancy. She raised her eyebrows questioningly at Gabe.

"Oh, what the Hell," he said. "At least we know what to expect there."

They rented two rooms, and agreed to meet in the lobby at seven in the morning. That would give them plenty of time to get to the Hearst Castle in time for the first tour at 8:00.

After the harrowing drive and prolonged nausea, Gabe was absolutely exhausted. He was asleep within ten minutes of entering his room.

At twenty minutes before 8:00 the next morning, Molly and Gabe turned off of the PCH and into the driveway entrance to the Hearst Castle. Although, the official sign actually read *Hearst San Simeon State Historical Monument*.

The visitor center set over one-half mile back and was not visible from the main road. Gabe was surprised when they reached the parking lot at the size of the building. The main house—the reason for the visitor center—was still another five mile drive up into the hills of the estate. Despite its distance from any major urban center, and difficult location along the coast (as evidenced by Gabe's terrifying car ride the night before), the historical site attracted over a million visitors every year.

William Randolph Hearst had been born into a wealthy family of privilege in San Francisco in 1863. His father had been a U.S. Senator, and his mother was a powerful public figure in her own right—especially for a woman in the early 20th Century.

Starting with one newspaper he took over from his father in 1887, Hearst bought additional papers and eventually created a media empire of newspapers, magazines, and even a movie studio. While he served two terms from New York in the U.S. House of Representatives, he lost many more elections than he actually won. Still, the man who controls the press controls the agenda, and Hearst became one of the most powerful men in the country. The Orson Welles classic movie *Citizen Kane* was a thinly veiled critique of his life.

He built the estate, which he called *La Cuesta*

Encantada (the Enchanted Hill), on land he inherited from his father. His original plan was to build a few small cabins at the top of the hill, but his plans quickly grew more grandiose. His mother was critical of the opulent construction plans, but when she died in 1919 during the great flu pandemic, he was free of her criticism to build as he pleased.

Between the years of 1919 and 1947, Hearst built his dream of *La Cuesta Encantada* (or as he usually called it—the ranch) with his favorite architect, Julia Morgan. What started as plans to build a small bungalow, turned into a huge main house accompanied by smaller guest houses, pools, gardens, an airstrip, and even a private zoo. By the time Hearst's health grew too frail to visit his "ranch" anymore, the main house (*Casa Grande*) had grown to over sixty thousand square feet with over fifty bedrooms.

Molly parked the car in the facility's parking lot, and they walked into the newly built visitor center. The center was huge and contained the ticket office for the castle tours, as well as several gift shops, a food court, a museum of the Castle and Hearst's life, and a large movie theater.

Gabe immediately headed to the "will call" ticket window to pick up their tickets for the 8:00 A.M. tour. He had ordered them yesterday online from his phone after Molly had announced they would be making the trip down to San Simeon.

The silver bouffant wearing ticket agent greeted them with a smile and a warm greeting of good morning. Gabe imagined that she had probably been here since the State of California turned the estate into tourist attraction in the 1950s.

"Excuse me, ma'am," Molly said politely. "My cousin works here, and I was hoping to surprise him if he was working today. His name is Trevor Hake."

The woman continued smiling at them. "Well, hon— let me check for you."

She walked away for a few minutes, then returned— smiling even more widely.

"You're in luck, hon," she said. "Your cousin Trevor is working today. He should be up at the main house gardens. Mention it to your tour guide, and I'm sure he'll help you find him."

She handed Gabe the two tickets, and directed them to a waiting area for their bus that would take them up to the estate.

"So, what do you think," Gabe whispered as they were walking away. "Do you think she knew old William Randolph personally?"

Molly slapped his arm in a playful manner.

"Let's just find this Trevor Hake and get him to tell us what he knows about my brother."

The bus which would transport them up the hill to the castle was a full size motor coach, as big as the average Grey Hound. From the visitor center, it was a twisting five mile drive up the hill on the narrow road. Gabe was unpleasantly reminded of the drive down the PCH last evening.

"You know," Molly said, breaking his train of thought. "I'm sure the bus driver runs this route at least ten times a day."

Gabe smiled. She could read him pretty well.

The nearly full bus unloaded its cargo of tourists in front of the main house. Gabe was struck by how ostentatious it all seemed. The architecture was a mix of Spanish, Middle Eastern, and native Californian. He was amazed that it was possible to get all the ornate materials necessary to build such a place up the small, winding road he had just traveled.

The tour guide corralled the bus passengers into a somewhat organized group, then began herding them up the huge set of marble steps leading from the driveway to the gardens in front of the house. The man began giving his well-practiced spiel about the life of William Randolph Hearst and his grand home.

Molly was only half listening; she was looking around for any workers who might possibly be Trevor Hake. But, other than their tour guide (who had introduced himself as "Martin" as they all exited the bus) she saw no other employees.

The tour was walking away from the Neptune Pool on their way into the main house, when Gabe grabbed her arm.

"Look over there," he said, pointing to a small garden area. "Does that look familiar?"

Molly squinted into the morning sun. It was the same Egyptian statue—the Sekhmet—that they had seen in the photos in Mark's office.

"It's the same statue, isn't it?"

"Yeah," Gabe said. "I'm pretty sure it is."

They pulled away from their tour group and headed toward the statue. There were actually twin Sekhmet statues, each propped on a pedestal over a small fountain. The fountain was tiled in Moorish ceramic, with inlays of a metallic looking substance.

A gardener was working nearby, and walked up to them as they were staring at the statues.

"Pretty amazing, huh? The man said approaching them. "They're probably the oldest things in the whole state of California."

Gabe nodded. "So, they're authentic pieces?"

"Oh, absolutely," the man said. "They were purchased from an excavation in Egypt in the the 1920s. My grandfather worked with Mr. Hearst's architect, and personally oversaw their installation here."

Molly opened her mouth to ask the man a question, when she looked down and noticed his name tag. It read *Trevor*.

CHAPTER 13

San Simeon, California (June, 1925)

For the life of me Miss Morgan, I cannot understand why you must always be so difficult," An exasperated William Randolph Hearst said.

"I'm sorry, Mr. Hearst," the petite woman said, looking up at her employer's face. "I'm really not trying to be difficult, but I feel very strongly that this is the right piece for the space."

At six foot three, Hearst towered over the female architect by nearly a foot and a half. Still, she stood her ground and made her argument to a man who would terrify most people—presidents and kings included.

"Miss Morgan, I employ professional art collectors for precisely these types of acquisitions. Why should I forgo their expert opinions for that of my architect?"

"Well, Mr. Hearst," Julia Morgan said quietly. "I believe you only should if you trust my vision for *La Cuesta Encantada.*"

Hearst sighed deeply. This woman always knew just what to say to him to steer him in her direction. Of course he trusted her vision for this special place—maybe even more so than his own.

"So, you say you have already found what you believe are the perfect pieces?"

"Yes, sir," She said, fully aware that she had already won this argument. "They are two sekhmet figures, pulled from a recent excavation near Giza."

Hearst nodded his head, and pretended to be further considering the issue. Of course, this was more for his ego than anything—he realized that nearly as soon as he had begun the argument he had already lost it.

"And you have a man who can make the acquisition?"

"Yes, sir. My associate Mr. Hake can leave almost immediately for Cairo. He can make the acquisition and personally accompany the pieces back to San Simeon."

"Ok, Miss Morgan," Hearst said. "But I insist that the pieces be fully installed by my Autumn party in October." Good—by making this demand, at least he still could retain some kind of control.

"Of course, sir," she said. "I will personally see to it."

With that, she turned and walked away; ready to put her plans into action to bring the three thousand year old statues from Egypt to California.

William Randolph Hearst shook his head. No matter how hard he tried, he could not understand how this woman could hold so much influence with him. Julia Morgan enjoyed a power with him that no other living woman could hold. Not even his mistress, the actress Marion Davies, and certainly not his wife.

Of course, he greatly respected her opinion, and maybe in some ways he was always looking to her for her approval. The only other woman that had ever made him feel this way was his mother—and she had been gone for nearly five years now.

If Joseph Pulitzer could see me cow-towing to a woman, he thought.

Less than three months later, William Randolph Hearst was standing in front of the two sekhmet statues, admiring their beauty. The pieces were striking, and were further enhanced by the fountains that his architect had designed. Standing in this small garden near the Neptune

Pool, he could almost imagine he was in ancient Egypt; a Pharaoh of his own kingdom.

And, as usual, Julia Morgan had been exactly right.

CHAPTER 14

Hearst Castle (Current Day)

T revor Hake?" Molly asked the gardener who had approached them.

Gabe saw the man's eyes go wide with surprise at being addressed by name. For a moment, he thought the man may try to bolt.

"Y-y-es," he stammered. "Who are you?"

"My name is Molly Newman. Mark Newman is my brother."

She waited a moment to judge any glimmer of recognition. She clearly saw it.

"My brother has gone missing. We found your name and number in his notes, and I'm hoping you may be able to help us find him."

He looked at her intently. "You're the FBI agent?" He finally said.

Gabe had a feeling that Trevor Hake was now grateful for not following his initial instinct and running.

"Yes, Mark mentioned me to you?"

"Briefly. Listen, I haven't seen Mark in a couple of weeks. I don't have any idea where he is."

"Well, maybe we can sit a while and talk. Maybe you know something that may help us and not even realize it."

Trevor Hake looked around nervously.

"Look, I've already been written up twice this month for being late. One more and I'm going to get my ass canned. Plus, Mark already screwed me over once—I helped him get a job here, then he only works a few shifts and never comes back again."

It was Molly's turn to look surprised.

"Mark worked here?"

"If you want to call it that," Trevor Hake said, then spitting in the dirt to his side.

At first Gabe noticed a look of anger coming to Molly's face, but it quickly faded. She took a deep breath and smiled slightly.

"Please, Trevor. We're really worried about Mark, and maybe you can help." She reached out and touched his forearm.

Gabe was surprised by her actions. Molly generally hated when a woman played on her feminine wiles with a man to help get her way. It showed him just how desperate she was to get some kind of lead on Mark.

"Ok," he said, softening to her approach. "I get off work at 3:00. Meet me down in the visitors center then. But I need to get back to work before my boss sees me talking to you."

With that, he quickly turned and walked away.

"So," Molly said after he was out of earshot. "What in the hell are we going to do for the next six hours?"

"Finish the tour, I guess," Gabe replied.

After the interaction with Trevor Hake, Gabe and Molly caught up with their group and finished the tour. Martin the tour guide had never even realized they were missing.

After the tour, they took the bus back down the hill to the visitors center. With several hours to kill, Gabe explored every square inch of the museum; skimmed through nearly every book in the gift shop, and watched the film on William Randolph Hearst's life three times. By the time three o'clock rolled around, Gabe felt he could probably write a pretty complete biography on William Randolph Hearst and his *La Cuesta Encantada*.

Gabe and Molly were sitting at a table in the food court when they saw Trevor Hake exit a door marked *Employees Only*. He saw them, and seemed simultaneously surprised and disappointed. Gabe imagined that he thought the idea of a six hour wait would have been too daunting for them. He obviously had never met Molly.

He walked up to the table facing them.

"So, you waited, huh?"

"Yes, Mr. Hake," Molly said. "I told you it was very important that we talk to you. I'm really concerned about Mark."

She motioned for him to sit down. He sat on the same side of the table as Gabe.

"Well, I guess you might as well call me Trevor. Mr. Hake was my Dad—I never quite earned that rank yet. What do you want to know? I gotta be at an AA meeting in a few hours, and it's court ordered."

Molly sat back in plastic molded chair and looked at him carefully. Gabe could tell that she was going into her law enforcement interrogation stance.

"Well, I guess first things first. How do you know my brother?"

"Mark found me online and sent me an e-mail. That was probably six months or so ago. He was real interested in the Castle and in Julia Morgan—the lady that built it."

The explanation did not seem to make much sense to Molly.

"No offense Mr. Hake—Trevor. No offense Trevor, but why would he contact someone on the grounds crew for information about the Hearst Castle? I'm sure there were lots of people on the museum staff he could have talked to?"

"Because, he knew who my grandfather was."

Gabe focused on that comment, and was immediately reminded of a caption from a photo he had seen in one of his many tours of the museum today. It was a picture of Julia Morgan during the construction of the Hearst Castle, and the caption had identified the man with her as *her trusted assistant, Walter Hake.*

"Walter Hake was your grandfather?" Gabe asked.

Molly was surprised by Gabe's question.

"I saw pictures of him in the visitor center's museum."

It was as much of an explanation to Molly as it was to Trevor Hake.

"Yeah," Hake replied. "My grandfather worked for Julia Morgan for almost forty years. The man practically worshipped that woman. My grandma always hated her though—she was always sure Miss Morgan was trying to steal her husband."

Molly smiled slightly at him and nodded for him to

continue.

"Of course," Trevor said with a grin. "I don't think grandma had anything to worry about—I don't think the lady was too interested in any man."

He ended the sentence with a wink. Molly's smile immediately disappeared, and Trevor Hake was perceptive enough to change his course of conversation.

At least he's not a complete idiot, Gabe thought.

"So, your brother wanted to know about a story that had been written in a biography of Julia Morgan. About how she had asked my grandfather to burn all of her papers on the day she retired."

"And," Molly asked. "What did you tell him?"

"I told him it was the truth. The crazy old bat had told Grandpa to burn all of her papers. And, he did it too—mostly anyway."

"Mostly?"

"Yes, he burned everything but her handwritten journals that Grandpa said she had written in ever since he knew her."

"What happened to the journals?" Gabe asked.

"After Grandpa died they went to my Dad. He worked for the Castle too—when he retired he was chief archivist for the historical monument."

"So, I'm assuming the journals became part of the

archive?" Gabe asked.

"Nope," Trevor Hake said simply. "He kept them in the family. No one associated with the Hearst Monument or the State of California ever knew we had them. I never even saw them until after he died, and I got them in his will."

"But, Mark knew?" Molly asked.

"He sort of put the pieces together, I guess. I tried to sell them a few years back on eBay, but the best bid I ever got was around $700. I figured they had to be worth more than that, so I held on to them."

"Where are the journals now?" Molly asked.

"I don't know. You'd have to ask your brother that—he bought them from me."

Molly narrowed her eyes, trying to determine if Trevor Hake was showing any signs of lying. She believed he was telling the truth.

"What was in the journals?" Gabe asked.

"A bunch of crap that didn't mean a damn thing to me—lots of notes about buildings and stuff. Drawings, weird looking jewelry, maps, a bunch of stuff."

"Maps of what?"

"I couldn't tell ya. Look, I never was interested in the same stuff my granddad and father were, and probably wouldn't understand it even if I was. To be perfectly blunt, I've been a fuck up pretty much my whole life. I think the only reason Dad left them to me was that there was nobody else in the family—he always acted like those things were made out of fucking gold."

"How much did Mark pay you for the journals?" Molly asked.

"Five thousand dollars."

Gabe's eyes grew wide. Mark must have believed that there was some very important information contained in those journals.

"So," Molly said, leaning in toward Trevor's side of the table. "Some stranger sends you a note on the internet and you're willing to sell off your family's most valued possession just like that?"

"Listen, lady, I don't need you to judge me. I already told you I'm a fuck-up, OK? For Christ's sake— my grandfather was the chief assistant to one of the most famous architects in the world, my father was the archivist of a museum, and got personal Christmas cards from the California governor—and I trim the fucking bushes. What do you want from me?"

Molly sat forward and slammed her fist down on the table between them.

"I want you to give me some information that I can use to find my brother!"

Gabe looked across the table at her, silently pleading

with her not to lose her cool. Molly, on the other hand, thought seeing a little anger from an authority figure might be just what Trevor Hake needed.

"Look, I'm sorry. I needed the money. I've had some run ins with the law, and even more with the local bookie. The only reason I've even got this crappy job is because of who my dad and grandpa were. Those journals meant a lot more to Mark than they did to me, and he had the money to pay for them."

For a moment, Gabe thought the man may actually begin to cry.

"You said Mark actually worked here?" Gabe said, attempting to change the subject ever so slightly from the emphasis on Trevor Hake's miserable life.

"Yeah. A few months after I had sent him the journals, he told me that he'd pay me another $2500 if I could help get him a job at the Castle. Said he didn't care what he did, just as long as he could be up at *Casa Grande*."

"And, you were able to help him get a job here?"

"Yep. Got him on as a part time fill-in guide. Basically, his job was just to hang around with the crowd and help out if there were too many questions for the leader guide to handle. Of course, he only worked for less than a week then never showed up again. Made me look like a real asshole with my boss."

Molly sat back against her chair again, dejected. She was afraid that this was going to be just another dead end to actually finding her brother. She was starting to stand up, and about ready to thank Trevor for his time and leave, when he made one additional comment.

"Maybe you should get the stuff out of his locker. Management's just gonna throw it all out anyway."

"His locker? He still has things here?"

"Yep, I can take you back to see it if you want."

Molly smiled very widely at Gabe. Maybe this would not turn out to be such a dead end after all.

CHAPTER 15

Hearst Castle (Current Day)

Trevor Hake got permission from the visitor center's operations manager to take Molly and Gabe back to the employee locker room with the single purpose of cleaning out Mark Newman's locker. The center's manager was pleased to have the locker cleaned out; he had new employees starting soon to ramp up for the busy season and he needed all the space he could get. Plus, if his sister was cleaning out the locker it would save him from having to do all the paperwork necessary when he disposed of a former employee's personal belongings.

Gabe guessed there were probably a few hundred half lockers; all containing the digital type of locking mechanism that was so common now in hotel safes. That meant each employee could specify their own custom combination; an additional level of personal security.

"I'm going to have to call down and find somebody with a master key," Trevor Hake said.

"Actually," Molly said walking toward the locker. "Let me try a combination real quick before you do that."

She walked up the locker and pressed several digits on the keypad. A few seconds later the locker beeped, and a green light emitted from what had previously been a red one.

"Let me guess," Gabe said. "*Rambo2* again?"

"Nope. It was 26-44-13. The same combination that was on his bike lock when we were kids. I don't think he ever figured out how his bike kept getting moved either."

Molly opened the locker. There were a few facility issued jackets with the Hearst logo on them, a blue name tag which read *Mark*, a few books about the art collection of the Hearst Castle (Gabe recognized them as ones he had seen earlier in the gift shop), and an empty coffee thermos.

Molly looked on the floor of the locker and found two plastic jugs which both seemed to contain some sort of powered substance. Both were hand labeled with magic marker on masking tape. One was labeled *zinc sulfite*, and the other said *ferrite dust*. Molly lifted the bottles up toward Gabe, and looked at him questioningly.

Gabe read the labels, and a look of recognition spread over his face.

"Trevor," he asked. "Is there any kind of night tour or

event that goes on at the castle?"

"Well, yeah. There's a night tour that goes on this time of year through Summer. In fact, that was the shift that Mark had asked to work."

Gabe smiled and nodded at him. He handed Molly the shopping bag that Trevor had given them to load up Mark's belongings, and she put the bottles and a few other items into the bag.

"Thank you very much for your help, Trevor," Gabe said, shaking the man's hand.

He pulled Molly by the arm, and began to lead her toward the exit door of the locker room.

"Where are you going in such a hurry?" She asked.

"We need to get to the box office."

"Box office?"

"Yes, before all the tickets for tonight's evening tour are sold out."

It was a few minutes before 7:00 in the evening, and for the second time that day Gabe and Molly rode the tour bus to the top of Hearst's *Enchanted Hill.* As the bus turned one of the many sharp corners, Gabe caught a glimpse of the giant orange sun sinking into the Pacific Ocean in the distance. It was beautiful.

"So," Molly said. "Run this idea by me one more time."

"When I saw those bottles of powder in Mark's locker, it made me remember an article I read awhile ago about unique chemical reactions," Gabe replied. "Zinc sulfide has phosphorescent properties, and it glows under blue or ultraviolet light. Ferrite dust is extremely magnetic—so much so that it even attracts to metallic surfaces underwater. It can be used to find metal objects in dark, isolated locations."

"So, mixing the two would create a magnetic dust that glows in the dark?"

"Well, at least that glows in blue light."

"And, you think the Egyptian statues are the reason Mark had these chemicals?"

"Yeah, that's my guess anyway. I noticed that the fountain basins were made out of tile, but with some magnetic flex mixed in—it was a very unusual design. I also noticed that the uplighting on the sekhmets had blue bulbs. At first I thought it must be for a cool nighttime effect, but then after we found the chemicals I started to think differently about it."

The evening tour was only offered during the peak tourist seasons, and was unique from the day tours in that it featured actors dressed in early Twentieth Century period clothing. It was designed to give tourists the feeling as if they were actual guests of William Randolph Hearst during the heyday of *La Cuesta Encantada*. The bus driver had warned his passengers that the actors were forbidden from breaking character during the course of evening.

They exited the bus in front of the same marble steps where they had been dropped off for the earlier tour. A man and a woman in 1920s period clothing was standing there to greet them.

"Good evening ladies and gentlemen," the man said in and exaggerated stage voice. "Mr. Hearst and Miss Davies have been expecting you. Please follow your guide to the Assembly Room for cocktails."

Gabe smiled. Molly rolled her eyes.

"What's sad," Gabe whispered. "Is that this is probably his dream acting gig."

"It's crap like this that makes me hate going to Disneyland."

"Well, that will all change once you become a mommy."

"Oh, no it won't," Molly replied. "I've already told Vickie that she has to take the kid to Disneyland—I'll hang out by the hotel pool."

Gabe smiled again. He wondered if Molly would still hold these same opinions after a few years of motherhood.

The tour group continued to walk toward Casa Grande, where they would enter the main living room (what Hearst had called the *Assembly Room*) through the large, ornate front doors.

"How do we separate ourselves from the herd?" Gabe whispered.

"Just follow along."

Just as they were about to walk into the large doorway, she dropped her bag off to the side and all of the contents came pouring out onto the ground.

"Oh, no!" She said, loud enough so that everyone would take notice. "Honey, help me pick up all of my stuff."

Their tour guide stood beside the door and smiled at them, he moved in their direction intending to help.

"Oh, we're fine," Molly said to him. "I don't want to hold up the tour by being such a klutz. We'll follow along in just a second."

The guide nodded, and walked through the doors after the last guest. The large ornate door closed softly behind him.

"See, that was easy."

They turned away from the main house, and headed toward the garden where they had seen the sekhmet statues earlier that day. The gardens were softly lit with landscape lighting, but the area around the Egyptian statues was unusually dark. Behind the foliage in the distant they could see a subtle blue glow.

The sekhmets bathed in blue light were quite striking in the early evening darkness.

"Wow," Gabe said impressed by the sight. "They look almost other-worldly in the blue light."

"I think they look a little creepy."

They walked up to the area immediately facing one of the statues, directly in front of the fountain.

"Hand me the bottles of powder," Gabe said.

Molly reached into her bag and pulled out both bottles of powder. She handed them to Gabe. He opened each bottle in succession, pouring a small amount of each powder into his hand and mixing it with his finger.

"How do you know how much to use?" Molly asked.

"I don't. I figure I'll give it a try and we'll adjust the amounts from there."

He opened his cupped hand and let the powder fall into the fountain. As soon as the blue light touched the dust, it immediately began to glow. The dust hit the water, and it was immediately and quickly pulled downward to the bottom of the fountain.

It took a few seconds for the dust to settle on the floor of the fountain, but when it did, there was a clearly visible sign. It read:

CLF

"CLF?" Molly said.

Gabe nodded, clueless as to what it meant as well.

He walked over to the second sekhmet and its fountain and performed the same tasks. Just as quickly, the glowing powder collected on the bottom of the fountain. This statue contained a message as well. It read:

09.527

Gabe used his cell phone camera to take photos of both messages, and jotted down a few notes. The glowing messages were already beginning to fade.

"Apparently, the glowing effect is only temporary," He said.

"So, what does it mean?"

"I don't have a clue. But, I'm pretty sure it must mean something significant. Either Hearst or Julia Morgan went to all the trouble to not only have this written in the fountains, but also to have it hidden like a code. Then Mark spends thousands of dollars to get the information necessary to read that code."

"But, it's still a code."

"Yep," Gabe said. "But a code can be broken."

She nodded in return, but not feeling as confident as Gabe.

"We should catch back up with our tour," Gabe said. "Before they realize we're missing and send the castle police after us."

They then spent the next few hours as the imaginary guests of William Randolph Hearst and Marion Davies.

CHAPTER 16

San Simeon, California (Current Day)

Molly awoke very early and had made a crack-of-dawn Starbucks run. When she returned, Gabe was already up and sitting at a table by the pool at the Motel 6, and was working on his laptop.

"There you are," he said smiling as he saw her approach. "When I saw the car was gone, I was beginning to think you had ditched me."

"Yeah, no such luck. I need your help too badly in figuring all this out."

"Well, if that would have been the case I guess there would be a lot worse places to get ditched."

The morning was bright and sunny, and the air was fresh and clean. Even the pool area at the cheap roadside motel seemed beautiful on a morning like this. Gabe was understanding why California had always been considered the promised land for so many people. He almost felt that way right now himself.

"So, crack the code yet?" Molly said, sitting down at a chair next to Gabe.

"I realize you think I'm some sort of genius or something, but I think this one is going to take a little while."

Molly nodded, and took a sip of her steaming coffee.

"I've been trying Internet searches so far, but not really finding anything solid or that makes sense. A search on CLF comes back with over ten million hits."

"Have you tried combining it with other search terms, like *Hearst Castle* or *Julia Morgan*?"

"Of course," Gabe replied, somewhat impatiently. "I've tried every combination I can think of. I did get some interesting results back on searching *CLF+Grand Canyon*."

"Really? What?"

"A press release from something called the Conservation Lands Foundation, praising the Interior Department for recently banning mining permits within the Grand Canyon."

Molly took another drink of coffee which was rapidly cooling in the morning air.

"Great. Let's look into it."

"To be honest, I think that would end up being a

huge waste of our time."

Molly looked at him silently; not liking the answer, but wanting to hear more of the explanation.

"I think the reference is way too new," Gabe said. "If what Trevor Hake told us is true, the statue installation—and the hidden code—has been there since the 1920s. We need to find a reference which fits better into that timeline."

Molly opened her mouth to begin making another comment, then abruptly stopped when something captured her attention in the motel's parking lot. She stared intently as a man parked his car, looked around, then came walking toward them.

"Oh, shit," Molly said.

"What's wrong?"

"It's my asshole partner."

A man that Gabe guessed to be in his late thirties walked up toward their table by the pool. He seemed pretty tall (at least he seemed tall to Gabe who was sitting), and was wearing a dark colored suit with a white shirt and red-patterned tie. He took off a pair of reflective Oakley's, and revealed what Gabe thought may be the greenest eyes he had ever seen.

"Agent Newman," the man said.

"You've got some hell of a nerve tracking me down here. I'm taking a few personal days, and that's not any of your concern."

The man shook his head.

"Molly, trust me—I wouldn't be bothering you if someone hadn't asked me to."

"The assistant director?"

"No. Vickie."

Molly's eyes opened wide, and her mouth hung open in surprise. It was not very often that Gabe witnessed her speechless.

"Vickie is really, really worried about what you're doing," the man continued. "And, she asked me to check up on you."

Gabe knew Molly well enough to know she was absolutely furious, but she was fighting the urge to show it. She did not want to give her partner the satisfaction.

"Well, as you can see, I'm perfectly fine. How did you even know where I was?"

"You've been using your credit card all up and down the California coast. I'm reasonably sure a first week cadet could have tracked you down."

The man turned to Gabe and extended his hand.

"Hi, we haven't been properly introduced. I'm Jarod McIntire."

Gabe returned the handshake.

"I'm Gabe Patrick—an old friend of Molly's."

"Well, Gabe, you certainly have my sympathies," Jarod said with a wink.

Gabe smiled at the remark. Molly rolled her eyes.

She was interrupted by her ringing cell phone. She looked down at the caller ID. It was Vickie.

"Excuse me," she said coldly, rising from the table. "This is a call I need to take."

As Molly walked away from the table, Jarod sat down in another chair at the table across from Gabe.

"So, has she always been such a joy to be around?"

"She's just worried about her brother, that's all."

"Maybe," Jarod said. "But, to be honest she wasn't all that fond of me even before her brother went missing."

"She takes a while to warm up to people, that's all."

"Yeah, ok," Jarod said laughing. "I'll let you stick with that one for a while."

Molly ended her call with Vickie and returned to the table.

"Molly, I really do want to help," Jarod said to her. "I talked to the assistant director, and he agreed to give us a few days to do some investigating. It's still not technically a bureau case, but that will give us a little leeway and some resources to poke around a little bit."

"And, what makes you think I need your help? Gabe and I are doing just fine."

"Come on, Molly," Gabe said. "We've kind of reached a roadblock here. If agent McIntire is willing to help us—"

"Call me Jarod."

Gabe smiled at him. For the second time in the last five minutes, Molly rolled her eyes.

"Ok," Gabe continued. "If Jarod is willing to help us, I think we should take him up on it. It's all about finding Mark, right?"

Molly swallowed hard and nodded. She knew Gabe was right, and for Mark's sake she needed to swallow her pride and accept her partner's help—regardless of how she felt about him personally.

"But," Jarod said. "I need you to come clean with me and tell me everything that's going on."

Over the next ten minutes, Molly and Gabe related to Jarod the story of their investigation so far, from their conversation with Dr. Schmidt and the notes in Mark's office, to the hidden code they discovered at the Hearst Castle.

"Wow, that's quite a story," Jarod said when they were finally finished. "So, what's our next step?"

"Our next step is to get to the Grand Canyon and start looking for Mark. He's been missing for almost a week at this point—we're running out of time."

"Molly, that's not nearly as easy as it sounds."

He reached into the messenger bag he was carrying

and pulled out several maps. He opened one of the larger ones.

"The Grand Canyon is absolutely huge—it covers thousands of square miles, most of it nearly uninhabitable."

He could tell from Molly's expression that she was not happy in the direction he was heading.

"He was last seen near Phantom Ranch, right?"

Molly nodded.

"That's practically in the center of the canyon with direct river access. He could have headed in nearly any direction from that point."

Gabe picked up one of the other maps that Jarod had placed on the table and began to look at it.

"This is kind of interesting," Gabe said.

Both Molly and Jarod stopped and looked at him.

"I never realized how strange some of the site names actually were in the Grand Canyon. *Buddha Temple*, the *Cheops Pyramid*, *Isis Temple*, the *Temple of Osiris*. Not exactly the Spanish or Native American names you'd expect in an Arizona canyon."

"Do you think that's relevant to finding Mark?" Jarod asked.

"Maybe. It seems a little coincidental that this whole thing started out with Mark attempting to prove the existence of Egyptian treasure in the Grand Canyon, and here are a bunch of landmarks named after ancient Egypt."

"So, let's start there," Molly said. "Let's pick one of them and go there, and if we don't find anything move on to the next one."

"Molly," Jarod said. "It's still a lot harder than that. I grew up in Arizona. Not only are these sites really remote—it could take days to hike or raft between them—but some of them are also in Government restricted areas. You need special permits just to get on the river, and those permits are booked years in advance."

"So, what's your solution? That we do nothing."

"No, I didn't say that. I just think we need to be smart about our next step."

Gabe was quiet for a moment, and appeared to be deep in thought.

"Jarod," he finally said. "The Grand Canyon is controlled by the National Parks Service, right?"

Jarod nodded.

"And, the Parks Service is under the jurisdiction of the Department of the Interior?"

Jarod nodded again.

"So, if we could get the permits from someone high up—say, the Secretary of the Interior—that would go a long way to helping us with what we need, right?

Jarod nodded again, but looked confused.

"Then, I think I know what our next step should be."

CHAPTER 17

San Simeon, California (Current Day)

Gabe explained to them that he had a prior history with Reginald Allard—the new Secretary of the Interior—and he might be able to convince him to give them some help. But, he believed that would require a quick trip to Washington, D.C. so that he could make that appeal in person.

Molly, who was anxious for action—any action—jumped at the opportunity to make some forward progress. She volunteered to scope out flights to D.C. Jarod said he would contact the assistant director in their office to alert him to their travel plans, and to get permission to travel under the auspices of the Bureau. That only left Gabe to somehow get a personal appointment on a day's notice with a member of the President's cabinet.

Each of the three went off to their own corners of the

Motel 6 pool area to follow through on their respective phone calls.

Gabe decided to take the most direct route first by calling the Department of the Interior. He was sure he would start out with a switchboard operator, but hoped that he could talk his way beyond that. Unfortunately, hope would not prevail.

"Good morning, my name is Gabriel Patrick. I'm a former colleague of Secretary Allard's, and I was hoping you might be able to patch me through to his office," he said with as much confidence as he could muster.

"I'm sorry sir," the Civil Service employee on the other end said. "I won't be able to connect you through to the secretary's office. However, you can contact him via our website."

While very polite, Gabe knew a brush off when he heard it. He also knew that the chances of Reginald Allard seeing something he posted on the department's website were somewhere between slim and none.

"Actually," Gabe said, attempting to sound more authoritative. "I'm arriving in D.C. tomorrow morning and I was hoping to get the opportunity to stop in and see my old friend."

Gabe was not completely sure, but he thought he heard the woman chuckle slightly on the other end of the phone.

"Sir, as I said—I'm unable to connect you to the secretary's office."

"Well, then—would it be possible for me to leave a message?"

"I can take the message, but I can't guarantee it will make it directly to the secretary or even his immediate staff."

"I understand, but I appreciate your assistance anyway. Please indicate that Gabriel Patrick called."

He spelled both his first and last names for the operator. Then he paused for a moment. He hated telling a blatant lie, but he knew that this was for a very good cause, and he could think of no alternative.

"Please let the secretary know that I was contacted by a reporter from Fox News who is aware of our former—," he paused for a moment, groping for the right word. "*Association.* I'm inclined to take the meeting unless the secretary could possibly find a few minutes in his schedule for me tomorrow."

"Is there anything else?" The woman's voice had now turned distinctly colder.

"Just my phone number. I can be reached at 614-555-7005."

He thanked the operator and hung up the phone. He had no idea whether or not his message would actually make it through to Reg or not. But, if it did, he was sure that the mention of a reporter snooping around a former colleague—especially when that colleague was Gabe—would get the man's attention.

He approached Molly and Jarod who had each finished their respective calls a few minutes earlier.

"I informed the assistant director of our plans, and he agreed we could continue," Jarod said.

Gabe wondered what Molly would have said and done if the assistant director's answer would have been in the negative. He was glad for both of their sake that he would not have to find out.

"Unfortunately," Molly said. "The travel situation isn't as easy as I'd hoped. The closest major—and I use the term *major* generously—airport is in San Luis Obispo. That's about an hour from here. But, every flight has at least two connections and requires a red eye through either Los Angeles or Chicago."

"I guess that shouldn't be too surprising," Jarod said. "We're sort of out in the sticks here. I had to sit in LAX all night to get in this early from Phoenix too."

Gabe realized that meant that nearly as soon as Jarod had gotten the call from Vickie, he dropped everything to come find Molly and help them. He looked closely at Molly, wondering if she was making the same realization. But, if she was, she was showing no indication of it.

That's why she's so good at poker, he thought.

"We can catch a flight that leaves San Luis Obispo at 6:00 P.M., take the red eye from LAX and get into Washington at 7:30 in the morning."

They all agreed that was the course they would follow. Gabe and Molly drove separately from Jarod to the airport since they had a rental car to return as well. Gabe tried to broach the subject of her relationship with her partner.

"You know, he really does seem to be a good guy, maybe you could use this opportunity to reboot your relationship…"

"Gabe," She said flatly. "Don't start this with me now."

They arrived in Los Angeles at a few minutes before 7:00 in the evening. Immediately upon landing, Gabe turned on his cell phone. He had one new voice message.

"Mr. Patrick," the female voice on the message said. "This is Allison Jenner. I'm a special assistant to Secretary Allard. The secretary received your message, and has cleared fifteen minutes on his calendar at 9:00 A.M. tomorrow to meet with you."

He heard the woman swallow hard on the recording, then continue.

"Mr. Patrick, the secretary also wanted me to tell you—and these are his direct words—you get fifteen minutes of his time and *if that isn't good enough you can try your luck to see if any damn reporter buys your story.*"

And with that, she had disconnected the phone.

Gabe smiled to himself. Old Reggie had not changed one bit.

CHAPTER 18

Washington, D.C. (Current Day)

Gabe, Molly, and Jarod exited the dimly lit jet bridge into the sun filled atrium of the main terminal at Ronald Reagan National Airport in Washington. Gabe squinted into the sun, and tried to force his eyes to adjust. He felt like crap. No matter how hard he tried, he could never sleep on airplanes, and that made it particularly hard on these overnight flights.

He looked at Jarod. If he was feeling awful from the time difference and the red eye flight, Jarod should feel twice as bad. After all, this was he second night of no sleep due to travel. But, if Jarod was feeling jet lagged and exhausted, he did a very good job of hiding it.

Must be that G-Man training, Gabe thought. He looked at this watch—it read 7:37 A.M.

"What time is your appointment?" Molly asked.

"Nine o'clock. And, his assistant was pretty clear that even if I was a minute late I'd forfeit my time."

"I suggest we take a cab then," Jarod said, joining the conversation.

Both Gabe and Molly nodded in agreement.

Since they had only carried on a small bag each, there was no reason to visit the luggage area. They followed the signs to ground transportation, then quickly found the signs pointing to the taxi stand.

Even for it being the height of rush hour on a Washington business day, the cab line was very short and they were climbing inside the backseat of a taxi within five minutes.

"The Department of the Interior," Gabe said to the cab driver. "Corner of C and 19th Streets, please."

"So," Molly said as they settled into the worn out leather upholstery. "You never quite explained to us how you could score an appointment with the new Secretary of the Interior on less than a day's notice."

"You're right, I haven't explained."

Gabe caught the raised eyebrow look that Molly passed to Jarod. Apparently, they could get along if the right situation presented itself.

"We used to work together," Gabe finally said. "At Ohio State."

"He was a professor with you at OSU?"

"Provost, actually. The art history department reported up through him. He was the reason my contract wasn't renewed, and I was summarily dumped. The next year he got the job as president at Indiana University, then Lieutenant Governor, then Governor of Indiana, and the rest is history."

"So," Molly said slowly, trying to measure her words. "You're asking the guy who fired you to do us a favor?"

"Yep, pretty much. Let's just say our relationship was *challenging*, and leave it at that."

However, Gabe could tell from yet another look that passed between his companions that they were not going to leave it at that.

"What went down between Reginald Allard and I at Ohio State has a much greater potential to harm him now than it does me."

Gabe did not look to see if Molly and Jarod were trading glances this time or not. He had said all he was going to say, and they would just have to be satisfied with that.

Traffic going into the District from the airport was heavy as Gabe had assumed it would be. The drive took nearly an hour, and they arrived at the corner of C and 19th at 8:45. As they exited the cab, Gabe handed the driver a fifty dollar bill and told him to keep the change.

The three stood on C Street facing the huge limestone building. Gabe glanced at his watch. They certainly were cutting this close.

"It's probably best that I go in alone," Gabe said.

Both Molly and Jarod nodded in agreement. The last thing either of them wanted was to be in the middle of an uncomfortable situation with their friend and a cabinet member.

"There's a little park across the street," Jarod said pointing. "We'll wait over there for you. That will give Molly a chance to go over the other notes with me that you found in Mark's office."

Gabe smiled, and tried not to act nervous, even though he really was.

"Well, here goes nothing."

He turned away from his friends and began a quick jog up the limestone steps leading into the Department of the Interior.

CHAPTER 19

Department of the Interior (Current Day)

Gabe was unpleasantly aware that he was sweating as he sat in a small waiting room near the secretary's office. He hated that this man could still have so much control over his self-confidence—even after all this time. He hated even more that he was here—proverbial hat-in-hand—asking this man for a favor.

If this would have just been about him, he never would have considered coming to see Reginald Allard. But, this was about Molly. She really needed his help and there was nothing he would not do to help her. Regardless of how personally humiliating it was.

Gabe had met Reginald Allard (or, who he liked to refer to as "Reggie" for no other reason than getting the man's goat) several years earlier. He had come in as provost as part of a new university presidential administration. At first Gabe did not pay the man much mind; he had been around academic bureaucracy his whole adult life and did not usually concern himself with the revolving door of administrators.

However, Reginald Allard was different. From their first meeting Gabe realized that he was not going to be able to just ignore this particular bureaucrat. This man had made it known that he planned to have active hand in all departments which fell into his area. Gabe might not have minded this so much if he would have believed the man had the background to run his department, but this man clearly did not.

He has a doctorate in zoology and natural history, he used to say to anyone who would listen. *What the hell does he know about fine arts programs?*

Gabe had always prided himself on his lack of patience for the bullshit of academic politics, regardless of how often his mentor Rudy had warned him it would be his ruin.

Liebchen, the old German used to say. *You must learn how to play the game. You don't have to like the game—but you must at least acknowledge it exists.*

Of course, he may as well have been talking to a brick wall. Gabe knew the political games existed—but he refused to play them.

The relationship between Gabe and his new boss continued to sour, especially as word got back to Allard about how he talked about him behind his back. The provost belittled him every chance he got, and never let Gabe forget that he could crush him anytime he wished. After one particularly unpleasant encounter, Gabe had had enough.

He had gone out with a few colleagues and drank considerably more than he should have. He complained about Allard all night, which he was sure his drinking companions would not hesitate to repeat as office gossip, but he did not care anymore. He went home, drunker than he had been in a long time, to write his letter of resignation.

However, instead of writing the letter, he started searching the Internet for mentions of his nemesis. He found an archived copy of the doctoral dissertation he had written over twenty years earlier on the origins of life on Earth. Working on a hunch, or for some other reason he never really quite understood, he copied the first paragraph of the document and pasted it into a search engine.

Hits were immediately returned, but instead of references to Reginald Allard's publication it came back to the work of another scientist who had written nearly the exact same words ten years earlier.

Gabe was emboldened. Had this man actually plagiarized his doctoral thesis? He searched for information and found the original author was a woman named Lucille Cooper who had died of breast cancer shortly after finishing her studies. She had attended Michigan State—the same university which Reginald Allard would attend for less than a year before transferring to West Virginia University.

This was almost too good to be true. He woke up early the next morning and contacted the library at Michigan State and requested a copy of Lucille Cooper's thesis. Then did the same thing for Reginald Allard's from West Virginia. Less than a week later, he held copies of both documents in his hands. They were nearly identical.

He called the provost's secretary and requested—actually, demanded—an appointment first thing the following morning.

Gabe walked into the provost's office the next morning with both documents in his briefcase. He wasted no time in slamming both down on his superior's desk and accused him of academic fraud. He then sat down in a chair facing his death, ready to enjoy seeing the man panic who had treated him so badly.

He was very disappointed.

Instead of panicking, or begging for Gabe to keep his secret, he instead sat back in his chair, locked his fingers behind his head, and smiled. Although, Gabe would remember later that while his mouth was smiling—his eyes were not.

"So, tell me Professor Patrick," Allard said slowly. "Exactly what end result do you think this is little show is going to get you?"

"It's going to result in a sham academic getting what he deserves," Gabe said defiantly.

"Really? And, what if I told you that I knew a few things about your history as well?"

Gabe swallowed hard and felt nervous. This was not at all they way he had pictured this meeting playing out.

"You've had several *relationships* with male graduate students who've reported to you over the years, haven't you?"

Gabe was angered by the way he said the word *relationships*.

"Listen, I never did anything wrong—any *relationships* I've ever had were between consenting adults."

"From near as I can tell, there have had at least five of those during your tenure at Ohio State. Sure, you say they were consensual, but are you so sure all of those young men would still say that? Especially if there were perhaps some promising opportunities for them at a major academic institution…"

"You're a fucking bastard!"

"Yes, I've been called that before—and, probably much worse. Listen Gabe, believe it or not I'm actually impressed that you were able to pull this all together and felt ballsy enough to challenge me like this. And, yes, you're right—you could do some serious damage to my career and reputation."

Gabe's mouth was dry and he felt as though he may pass out. How could this have gone so wrong, so quickly?

"But, Gabe," Allard said in a hissed whisper. "I will absolutely fucking destroy you. When I'm done with you no college would hire you to work in the cafeteria, let alone teach again."

Gabe tried to swallow but could manage no moisture in his mouth. This was quickly becoming a nightmare.

"So, here's what we're going to do. Your contract is up at the end of the academic quarter, and it will not be renewed. You'll leave the university and we'll both forget what we know about each other."

But, Gabe could not forget. He called Rudy that night to tell him what had happened.

I'm sorry liebchen—I truly am, Rudy had told him. *You're better to let this go…walk away and lick your wounds. You can return to fight another day.*

As far as Gabe was concerned, that day had finally come.

He would never forget Reginald Allard's last words to him.

Remember, mutual destruction is still destruction, Professor Patrick.

Professor Patrick.

Gabe startled from his daydream.

"Professor Patrick," the young woman said from the doorway.

He had not been called that title for a long time.

"Professor Patrick, the secretary can see you now."

Gabe stood up and followed her into the Secretary of Interior's private office.

CHAPTER 20

Office of the Secretary of the Interior (Current Day)

When Gabe walked into the office, Reginald Allard was on the phone. He snapped his fingers and pointed at a armchair facing his desk.

He's still a bastard.

Gabe sat in the chair facing the man who was eighth in line to the Presidency of the United States. Allard ended his phone call, hung up the phone, than sat there staring at Gabe.

"You have five minutes," He said coldly.

"Thank you for seeing me, Reginald. I really appreciate your time."

"Mr. Secretary."

"Excuse me?" Gabe said perplexed by the statement.

"I'm a senior member of the President's Cabinet. You

will address me as Mr. Secretary," he said as coldly as before.

"Of course. *Mr. Secretary*."

Yes, he was definitely still a bastard.

"Mr. Secretary, I need your assistance with a personal matter. My good friend—an FBI agent, by the way—has been alerted her brother has gone missing in the Grand Canyon."

Reginald Allard continued to stare at him, but still said nothing.

"As I'm sure you're aware, access to the Colorado River in the Grand Canyon requires special permits. There's a long wait and a lottery system to obtain one, but you can personally issue any park permit with a stroke of your pen."

Reginald Allard sat back in his chair, and the edges of his lips turned up in what Gabe assumed was an attempt at a smile.

"So, you threaten me with blackmail because you want to go on a boat ride?"

"Reg—*Mr. Secretary*. Please-this is literally a matter of life and death."

"If this man's sister is an FBI agent, why isn't the bureau taking the lead in this case? That seems like a more natural choice for her to go to for help, rather than an art history professor."

"*Former* art history professor. But, the FBI doesn't believe they have jurisdiction. They say it's a matter for the

Parks Service. Which, is what brings me to you."

"So, you tried blackmailing me before and it pretty much ended up ruining your life. Why put yourself through that again now?"

"Because," Gabe said. "Things have changed now. Whatever dirt you thought you had on me no longer has any power to hurt me. I have a new career; I have a new life. I'm a different person today."

"And, if I give you what you're asking for?"

"I thank you profusely, and you never have to see or hear from me again."

"And, if I don't?"

"I call the reporter from Fox News and I give him proof that the new Secretary of the Interior plagiarized his doctoral thesis off a dead woman. The president will be up against a tough election next year—do you really want to become that kind of a distraction to the administration?"

Gabe was sure that if looks could kill, Reginald Allard would have caused his death in that very instant.

"And, how do I know you won't show up here six months from now, shaking me down for something else?"

"Because, I give you my word that I won't. To be honest, I can't ever imagine you having anything I'd ever need again."

Gabe regretted the last statement nearly as soon

as it came out of his mouth. Pissing Reginald off would do nothing to help his cause.

Without a word, Allard stood up from behind the desk and walked out the office, closing the door behind him. Gabe had no idea where he went, or what he should do now. Several minutes went by and he was fully expecting someone to come in and escort him out, when the door opened and Allard returned. He started to hand a manilla envelope to Gabe, then abruptly pulled it back.

"I want one thing," he said.

"What?"

"I want you to send me the copies of the thesis that you have. Mine—and the other one."

Gabe nodded in agreement, and Allard handed him the envelope.

"These permits will give you the permission and clearance necessary."

"Thank you, Mr. Secretary. Thank you so much."

He reached out his hand in an attempt to smooth over bad feelings he had carried around for far too long. Reginald Allard refused his hand in return. Instead, he turned and walked out of the room again.

Thirty seconds later, the woman who had escorted Gabe into the room was there to escort him out.

Gabe felt as though a huge weight had been lifted from his shoulders as he walked out of the front doors of the Stewart Lee Udall building which housed the Department of the Interior. He bounded down the marble steps and straight across C Street, narrowly missing being hit by a car.

He crossed the street and entered Triangle Park. He looked around and nearly immediately saw Molly and Jarod sitting on a stone bench toward the middle of the park. Both seemed heavily engrossed in the folder of notes they had printed from Mark's office in San Francisco.

He walked up to them in a pace that was closer to a slow jog than a walk.

"Well?" Molly asked as she saw him approach.

"I got the permits," Jarod said holding up the manilla envelope.

"Jesus," Molly said smiling. "Exactly what kind of dirt do you have on this guy?"

Gabe returned the smile but said nothing. While he despised the man, he intended to keep the promise he had made to Reginald Allard. He sat down on the bench next to Jarod.

"So, what have you two been working on?"

"We've been going through the notes you and Molly

found in Mark's office," Jarod said.

"Any luck?"

"Not really," Molly said. "We've been focusing on the note which said *Freer 16 gal*, but we can't find any references that make sense."

Jarod nodded in agreement.

"Yeah, we've pretty much hit a wall on that one," Jarod said. "We're pretty sure it has to be some sort of liquid—hence the *gallons* description—but we can't find any substance called *freer*, or even anything close to that."

Gabe had been thinking about the note since they had found it as well, and had made just as little progress.

"Then," Molly said. "There's all these pictures of jewelry and art. Most of it looks Egyptian."

Art. That caused Gabe to consider something else.

"Hey," he said. "What were the letters we found in the fountain at Hearst Castle?"

Molly looked back through her notes.

"The letters were *CLF*," she said.

Gabe pulled out his phone and began to type some characters into its web search engine. Within a few seconds he had several valuable hits.

"Well, I'll be damned," Gabe said.

"What?" Molly and Jarod both exclaimed at the same time.

"*CLF* could stand for *Charles Lang Freer.* He was an industrialist who gave his vast art collection to the Smithsonian to start an art museum named after him. Freer's speciality was ancient cultural art—including Egyptian."

Both Molly and Jarod were pleased that this clue was finally taking some sort of path.

"What were the numbers written in the other fountain?"

"*09.527*," Molly said.

"That fits the numbering system the Smithsonian uses to catalog its collections," Gabe said. During the hunt for Rudy's murderer and the missing relic, he became very familiar with the Smithsonian's ways of doing things.

"Maybe *Freer 16 gal* actually means gallery sixteen in the Freer museum—not a measurement of gallons."

"That's great," Molly said. "How long will it take us to get to this Freer museum?"

"I guess that depends on how fast you walk."

Molly and Jarod both looked at him questioningly.

"It's right on the National Mall," Gabe continued. "It's less than a mile from here."

CHAPTER 21

Freer Gallery of Art (Current Day)

Gabe discovered Molly could indeed walk very fast when it suited her. Less than twenty minutes later they were standing in front of the Smithsonian's Freer Gallery of Art on the National Mall.

Located on the Mall between the original Smithsonian "Castle" and the extremely popular Air and Space Museum, the Freer Gallery was the less famous little brother of these other museums. The gallery had opened in 1923 and was built in the Italian Renaissance style. It was constructed of granite and marble, and its design was inspired by the palazzos of Italy, where the museum's namesake had visited often.

The Freer Gallery was unique in that it was the first Smithsonian facility to be dedicated to the fine arts. It

171

was also the first institution museum to be created from an individual collector's bequest.

Freer had made his fortune manufacturing railroad cars in Detroit, and was one of the largest private art collectors of his day. With no immediate heirs to bequeath his vast collection, Freer decided to donate it to the people of the United States. The Freer Gallery of Art cost over one million dollars to build, and Charles Lang Freer personally paid for every penny.

Gabe, Molly and Jarod walked up the few marble steps to the front doors of the museum. Entering into small lobby, Gabe immediately noticed how quiet it seemed inside, especially compared to some of the busier museums—such as Air and Space or the Museum of the American Indian. In fact, the noise and crowds of the American Indian museum was the only thing that had saved him from a killer's wrath the last time he had been in this city.

The Freer museum was divided into multiple galleries, each one specializing in a different ancient culture's art. There were galleries for Chinese, Indian, Southeast Asian, Muslim, and Egyptian art, as well as some early American pieces. The galleries were arranged around the building in a square, with an outdoor courtyard occupying the center of the space.

A security guard standing behind a small desk just

inside the door nodded at them and smiled. She motioned for them to step over so that she could check the bags that all three carried. Gabe imagined she didn't see much action in this particular assignment.

After having their bags checked for potential dangers, Gabe walked over to a large map of the museum on the wall and studied it closely.

"The Egyptian collection is in gallery sixteen," he said.

Molly and Jarod both nodded in understanding. So far, the pieces seemed to be fitting together.

They walked immediately back to gallery sixteen, which was located on the opposite side of the building from the entrance. They bypassed the other galleries as they went. Gabe had been here several times before, and Molly would not have been interested anyway. He wondered if Jarod would be. Gabe realized that several times so far today, he had wondered how Jarod would think or feel about one subject or another.

The three entered gallery sixteen, and each headed in a different direction to quickly search the exhibits. The Egyptian gallery was comprised of two small rooms, and there were only five other visitors in the area at time.

Gabe was looking at a pair of stone falcons which dated from the Ptolemaic dynasty, when he heard someone whispering his name. He looked across the room; it was Jarod attempting to get his attention. There was something about the atmosphere of a museum which always encouraged people to whisper, even if the room was nearly empty.

Gabe walked over to the display case where Jarod was standing. It contained multiple amulets of various styles and sizes. Jarod pointed to one in particular. Gabe read its description.

The Wisdom of Isis

Date and origin unknown. Gifted to the Freer Collection, 1909.
09.527

"Is that what we're looking for?" Jarod asked.

"It certainly looks like it."

By that time, Molly had walked over and joined them.

"Is this it?"

Both Gabe and Jarod nodded.

It was a round amulet, which looked to be made out of bronze. The front surface of the disk was uneven and bumpy. There was a thin line of a blue gem encrusted into the surface, which Gabe assumed to be lapis. The blue jeweled line twisted and turned across the face of the amulet, but seemed oddly hap-hazard. About one-third from the top of the disk, a large red garnet overlapped the blue line.

"So, what does it mean?" Molly asked.

Gabe shrugged his shoulders, but continued to look at the amulet. There was something that seemed oddly familiar about it. Then, it occurred to him.

"Jarod," he said. "Do you still have that map of the Grand Canyon we were looking at by the pool yesterday?"

Jarod reached into his messenger bag and searched for the map. He handed it to Gabe, who stared at it intently. He alternated his gaze between the paper in his hands and the amulet in its case. Then, he pulled out his cell phone and snapped several pictures of the amulet.

"So, what is it?" Molly asked again. It irked her that Gabe was obviously on to something, but failing to share the information.

"I think," Gabe said quietly. "I think it's a map."

CHAPTER 22

Freer House, Detroit, Michigan (1909)

Charles Lang Freer was very surprised when it was announced that he had a visitor. He was even more surprised when he was told who the visitor was.

A young female architect from San Francisco—a woman named Julia Morgan—had arrived at his home a few minutes ago asking to speak to him regarding a very important matter. To his surprise, Freer realized that he had actually heard of Ms. Morgan. As an avid art collector he also had a keen interest in architecture. And, this young woman was making quite a name for herself in that realm. Not only had she designed several significant buildings on the west coast, but she was also the favorite architect of William Randolph Hearst—one of the most powerful men in the country.

Generally, Charles Lang Freer was not intimidated by powerful men. After all, most would consider him to rather formidable as well. However, William Randolph Hearst was in a completely different class than Freer.

Charles Lang Freer had little formal education, but had always been interested in the more scholarly pursuits of art and poetry. He was one of Michigan's wealthiest residents, having founded one of the largest railroad car manufacturing companies in the country.

He had begun seriously collecting art several years ago, after being told by his doctor that he should find a hobby to reduce the stress of his business life, and to improve his health. He became fascinated with fine art, especially the works of the American artist James Whistler. He and Whistler became very close, drawn together by a mutual interest in fine art.

He was also very interested in the art of ancient cultures. He traveled to Japan, Korea, Egypt, China, and India searching for and acquiring new items for his collection. By the early 1900s he had built one of the most valuable private art collections in the world.

Freer was never married and had no heirs, and he became increasingly concerned about what would happen to his art collection after he died. For that reason he decided to donate the entire collection to the Smithsonian to begin a museum of the fine arts. In addition to the collection, he also pledged all the funds necessary to build a gallery of his own design.

For this generous gift, Freer only asked for one thing—that he maintain full curatorial control over the collection for the rest of his life. Freer felt this was a very minor proviso to request, considering the generosity of his gift. However, Samuel Langley, the director of the Smithsonian was at odds with that proposal.

Langley absolutely refused the gift on behalf of the institution. He declared he would never have the collection of one of his museums dictated by some uneducated robber baron—regardless of how valuable that robber baron's offer may be. He refused the offer, that is, until he was overruled— by the President of the United States.

Freer had been acquainted with Theodore Roosevelt for many years, since the latter had been governor of New York. He was not in the habit of asking for personal favors, especially from the President of the United States, but he honestly felt he had no other alternative. Samuel Langley simply refused to listen to reason, and his stubbornness was going to cost the Smithsonian a treasure of immeasurable value.

So, Charles Lang Freer approached Roosevelt and made his case directly. Within a week Samuel Langley was directly ordered by the President of the United States to accept Freer's generous donation and establish the Freer Gallery of Art. Later, Freer would also personally commission portraits of Roosevelt and his wife Edith.

There was a short knock at the door to his study.

"Come in," he said.

The door opened and his housekeeper entered first, followed by a woman that Freer guessed could have been no more than five feet tall. She was a slight creature; barely larger than a teenage girl, Freer thought. As he stood from behind his desk, she walked toward him smiling.

"Mr. Freer," she said pleasantly. "I'm so sorry for dropping in unannounced. I'm so grateful that you agreed to see me."

He motioned for her to sit in a large leather chair facing his desk, and simultaneously dismissed the housekeeper from the study.

"Well, I must say I was quite surprised when I was told you were here to see me. But, I'm familiar with your work and am very impressed by your designs."

While ever so subtle, Freer believed that he saw the young woman blush.

"So, Miss Morgan," he said. "What could I possibly do for you that Mr. Hearst cannot?"

Julia Morgan liked a man who got to the point

quickly. It was a characteristic she found particularly admirable. Mr. Hearst shared that same trait.

"Sir, I request your assistance on a very important matter. There is an expedition currently being planned by the Smithsonian Institution which will have a horrible effect on a group of people. I'm asking for your help to use your influence with the Institution to put a stop to it."

To put it mildly, Freer was very surprised by the answer to his question.

"Miss Morgan, I'm flattered that you seem to think I might have such pull, but I assure you I'm only a grateful benefactor to the Smithsonian."

"With all due respect sir, you've made the single most important donation ever to the Smithsonian. They will listen to you even if they will listen to no one else."

Freer smiled and nodded slightly. This woman was clearly flattering him. However, she was not being unsuccessful in her attempt.

"Tell me about this expedition you wish to stop."

Julia Morgan felt encouraged.

"There was recently a front page article in an Arizona newspaper describing a recent discovery of Egyptian treasure in a cave in the Grand Canyon…"

"Egyptian treasure?" he exclaimed, sitting forward to the edge of his seat.

"Yes, sir. That's what the article reported. It also said that the Smithsonian is planning an expedition, led by a Professor S.A. Jordan."

"I can't believe the institution would waste its resources on something so preposterous. But, Miss Morgan, what interest do you have in stopping this expedition?"

"There's a group of very special people who inhabit this particular area of the Grand Canyon. Intrusion by the government would destroy their way of life."

"Indians?"

"I believe that's as good as description as any, sir."

Freer sat back in his chair. He picked up his pipe from an ashtray on his desk and lit it. He took a deep breath of smoke and exhaled it into the air above him.

"Why do you believe I'm the man to assist you in this endeavor?"

"Mr. Freer, your respect for the culture of ancient peoples is well known. Your work preserving the art of Asia, India, and Egypt is greatly admired."

Freer took a another deep drag of his pipe. He knew he was being pandered to, but for some reason he did not really mind it.

"Plus," she said looking him directly in the eye. "I have a donation to your collection as a token of my appreciation."

Freer's ears perked up. He always found it very difficult to refuse the inclusion of any new item to his precious collection.

Julia Morgan reached into her handbag and pulled out a small object wrapped in a white handkerchief. She gingerly unwrapped the item and handed it across the desk to Freer. He reached out and took it just as gingerly.

He tried to conceal his astonishment while looking at the item, but he was quite sure that he did not fool Julia Morgan for a moment. The item was a round amulet, around four inches in diameter. It appeared to be made of bronze, and was adorned with gems.

"Is this blue inlay sapphire?" he asked.

"Lapis, I believe."

"It's beautiful. Is this from the site in the canyon that you're seeking to protect?"

She nodded.

"What makes you think that I wouldn't believe that such a site should be explored?" he asked. "After all, if there are more items like this…"

"Because, sir," Julia Morgan said interrupting him. "From all I've learned about you, I know that you would never want to see harm come to a culture that could create an item like this. And, I guarantee you that if the Smithsonian is to proceed with this expedition, their culture will not only be harmed—it will be destroyed."

Freer looked at her closely. He did not believe he had ever seen a woman quite so serious about her intentions.

"Well, Miss Morgan, you make quite the compelling case. What exactly do you propose for me to do?"

"Sir, I only ask that you try to stop the expedition."

"And, if I fail?"

"Then I thank you for your effort, and pray for the best I suppose."

Freer emptied the smoldering remnants of his pipe into the crystal ashtray on his desk. He opened his desk drawer and dropped the gift from Julia Morgan into it. He stood again from behind his desk and extended his hand to her.

"Miss Morgan, you have told a very compelling story. I will do my best to honor your request."

"This is completely unacceptable," Professor Stephen Jordan said to the director. He had at first been pleasantly surprised by this unexpected visit from Samuel Langley, but the pleasantry had disappeared quickly.

"Professor, I'm very sorry. But the institution must cancel the expedition to the site in the Grand Canyon. That is the directive from the highest authority."

Jordan was simultaneously confused and furious. Ever since receiving the mysterious items from his colleague at the Tempe Normal School, he had thought of nothing but this expedition.

"Sir, this makes no sense. Why does the Smithsonian exist, if not to conduct research expeditions such as this?"

"I know, Stephen, I know."

For what it was worth, Langley really did hate delivering this news to one of his best archeologists. He hated even more that this was yet another directive coming to him from the President—by way of Charles Lang Freer.

"We have an important research project being conducted at Stonehenge with the British. I want you to lead it."

Jordan nodded. He was disappointed, but he knew this situation was out of both his and the director's hands. Maybe things will have changed when he returned from England.

Two weeks later, in the middle of a terrible storm, the ship carrying Professor S.A. Jordan and the rest of the Smithsonian team bound for England went down in the

North Atlantic. There were no survivors, and the ship and its passengers were never found.

CHAPTER 23

Washington, DC (Current Day)

Gabe could hear the subtle sound of running water in a fountain somewhere in the distance. He, Molly and Jarod were sitting on a set of stone benches in the sunny courtyard in the middle of the Freer Gallery. Gabe had his notebook computer sitting on his lap and was staring intently at it.

"Care to fill us in on what you're looking at?" Molly asked impatiently.

"Yes, of course," Gabe said. He had not even realized he had been ignoring them for the last twenty minutes or so. "I'm overlaying the photos I took of the amulet on my phone with an online map of the Grand Canyon…"

Molly waited for a moment, expecting him to continue.

"And?" She said, when he did not.

"And, I think we were right. The inlay line of the blue gemstone almost matches the flow of the Colorado River in the Grand Canyon exactly."

"What about the red stone?" Jarod asked.

"It seems to correspond very closely with a location on the map called the Temple of Isis."

Jarod looked at his paper copy of the map of the Grand Canyon.

"That's in a pretty remote location. It wouldn't be easy getting there."

"Who cares?" Molly said. "At least that gives us some direction to go in now."

Jarod opened his mouth to begin to say something else, when he caught eye contact from Gabe. He closed his mouth again before speaking. Gabe was right—trying to reason with her right now would not get them anywhere. It was interesting how a simple look could tell you so much.

"What was other note we found in Mark's office?"

"It just says *B Honantewa*," Molly said.

Gabe stared even more intently at his computer screen.

"There doesn't seem to be anything on the map that matches that term."

"Hmm," Jarod said, nearly under his breath.

Both Molly and Gabe looked at him. Molly raised her

eyebrow questioning.

"I wonder if that means Betty Honantewa?"

"Is that a name I should be familiar with?"

"Probably not," Jarod said. "Especially since you didn't grow up in Arizona in the 1970s. Betty Honantewa was a professor at the University of Arizona and was considered quite the political radical in her day. She staged a lot of protests for Indian rights—her group even chained themselves to the governor's mansion once. Remember that Oscars ceremony that Marlon Brando boycotted and had that Indian woman take his place?"

Both Gabe and Molly nodded in the affirmative.

"The rumors always were that Betty had organized that whole thing."

"Where is she now?" Gabe asked.

"I'm not sure. I haven't heard her name for years. She is a Hopi, so she might have gone back to the reservation. The Hopis have always tended to stay off on their own."

Gabe typed the name Betty Honantewa into the internet search engine, and was rewarded with hundreds of references.

"The most recent stuff I can find on here is from the early eighties," he said, clicking through the pages. "Nothing very recent. It's like she disappeared after 1983."

"Well, if the FBI can't find where she is, no one can,"

Molly said, looking through her purse for her cell phone.

"Molly," Jarod said. "Before we involve the bureau in this this, give me a chance to try something else first. I've got a friend in the Flagstaff Police Department. Let me give him a call first."

Molly nodded, but looked skeptical. Gabe found himself wondering what Jarod's definition of *friend* was.

Jarod pulled out his cell phone and walked away, leaving Gabe and Molly sitting alone on the stone benches. Gabe watched him as he walked away.

"*Christ,*" Molly said, rolling her eyes.

"What?"

"You like him don't you?"

"Of course, I like him. He's a nice guy, and I'll remind you he has dropped everything to help us find *your* brother."

"That's not what I mean, and you know it."

Gabe felt a little angry, and even more embarrassed. He opened his mouth to respond, but found he could not really think of anything to say. So, he just found himself just sitting there—turning deeper shades of red by the second.

"Of course. You would just have to develop a crush on my nemesis."

"You know, I think you might use that word nemesis way too often and too freely…"

He stopped speaking when Jarod began to approach them again. He motioned for Molly to be quiet as well. Again, she rolled her eyes.

"Well," Jarod said, walking up to them. "My friend on the Flagstaff PD says that Betty Honantewa has been living on the Hopi reservation for the past twenty years or so. She's still active in tribal politics, but doesn't do much with the outside anymore."

"So, how do we find her?" Molly asked.

"My friend says she's living in the village of Old Oraibi on the reservation. I guess our best bet is to go there and try to talk to her."

"Why can't we just call her? Try to save some time…"

"The Hopi aren't like the other tribes," Jarod explained. "They never got into the casinos, or marketing themselves as a tourist attraction for the white people. They keep to themselves. Hell, they don't even like mixing with the Navajo, and their reservation is surrounded by them. Even if we could reach her on the phone—which I doubt—it's really unlikely she'd talk to us."

"And, what if this is just some wild goose chase? We'd be wasting valuable time that Mark doesn't have. I say we forget about Betty what's-her-name and just go straight to that Isis place in the canyon."

"Molly, I think we should trust Jarod on this one," Gabe said.

She looked at him coldly. *Of course you'd say that,* her eyes seemed to say.

Gabe tried to ignore her scathing look.

"We found her name in Mark's notes. Plus, the Hopis have thousands of years of history in the Grand Canyon. It makes sense that if Mark was looking for something specific, he would seek her out to try to find answers."

Molly sighed loudly. "Ok, so how the hell do we get there?"

"It would probably be best to fly into Phoenix. It would be a lot easier to get a direct flight from Washington. Plus, my car is at the airport there."

"How far is it from Phoenix to her village?"

"I don't know—maybe four and a half or five hours? The roads aren't the best once you get past Flagstaff."

Molly seemed to be considering his proposal, but in her mind she already knew it was the only alternative. She just wanted to feel like she had some semblance of control for a moment.

"Ok. Let's do it."

Before she had even finished the sentence, Gabe was on his laptop keyboard tapping away and searching for three tickets to Phoenix.

CHAPTER 24

Phoenix Sky Harbor Airport (Current Day)

Although expensive, the three were able to get a direct flight from Washington to Phoenix on U.S. Air. They touched down at Sky Harbor Airport at a little before three in the afternoon, Arizona time.

The flight had been mostly empty (something that was becoming quite a bit of a rarity, Gabe noted), and they had been able to spread out on the plane and get some rest. Gabe had not done this much traveling since he and Kevin had been on the search for the Tzohar—and Rudy's killer. The jet lag was starting to catch up with him. At least this quest had not required an international flight—well, not yet anyway.

None of them had checked any baggage, so they were able to exit the plane and head straight to the ground transportation area of the terminal. They caught the shuttle bus to the remote lot where Jarod had left his car. Within twenty minutes of landing they were piling into Jarod's black Range Rover.

"Expensive car for a G-man," Molly said snidely.

"Used to be anyway," Jarod said, returning none of the snideness in which the comment had been offered. "It's eleven years old and has nearly 150,000 miles on it."

Gabe was impressed at Jarod's ability to deflect Molly's clear intention to antagonize him. That was a skill he might find useful as well.

A few miles outside of the airport, they entered Interstate 17 heading North to Flagstaff. A green highway mileage sign proclaimed Flagstaff to be 199 miles from their current location.

"Isn't Flagstaff near the Hopi Reservation?" Molly asked. "If Flagstaff is less than two hundred miles away, why is it going to take us five hours to get there?"

Gabe leaned forward from his perch on the backseat of the SUV so that he could better hear the conversation.

"Yeah, it's close. But, getting to Flagstaff is the easy part—all four lane highway to there. It's after we leave Flagstaff that it gets interesting."

"Difficult road?" Gabe asked from the backseat, inserting himself into the conversation.

"For some parts of it, road is probably too generous of a term. Nothing more than a wide desert trail in a lot of areas."

"Well, great," Molly said. "Let's hope your junker can make it there in one piece."

"Junker?" Jarod said laughing. "Just a little while ago you were criticizing me for having too expensive of a car!"

"Yeah, well I reserve the right to change the focus of my criticism."

Gabe caught just the faintest glimpse of a smile coming from Molly—more from her eyes, than her mouth. But, a smile none-the-less. Despite her every effort not to, Gabe could tell that Molly was softening her attitude toward Jarod.

"So, what do you know about the Hopi Reservation?" Gabe asked.

"Not a whole lot of personal experience, actually. I was up there a few times when I was a state trooper..."

"Wait," Molly said, interrupting. "You were an Arizona State Trooper?"

"Yeah, sure—I thought you knew that. What do you think—I just landed a gig with the FBI right out of high school?"

Gabe leaned forward a little more from the backseat, looking directly at Molly and waiting for her reaction. She said nothing, but Gabe noticed her face was looking a little redder than it had a few seconds before. This was obviously news to her—she had told Gabe that one of her biggest complaints about Jarod was that he had been handed a position in the FBI due to his father's connections. This news about him working his way up the ranks as a state trooper threw a bit of a wrench into that theory.

If Jarod noticed any sort of discomfort in Molly's demeanor, he did not acknowledge it. Instead, he just continued speaking.

"But, other than those few times I haven't spent much time there. The Hopi don't exactly welcome outsiders with open arms. In fact, you have to check in with the tribal center just to visit the reservation."

"Still hold a grudge, huh?"

Gabe cringed at the comment. For all of her wonderful qualities, Molly could come out with some of the most inappropriate comments sometimes. However, if that bothered Jarod, he certainly did not let it show.

"I don't think it's a grudge so much, but rather the Hopi are just very immersed in their own culture. Most of the other tribes—the ones in the East and Navajo particularly—have assimilated much more into American society. The Hopi like to keep with their old ways. They're still trying to live their lives as if the white man had never shown up on their doorstep."

"Betty Honantewa lives in Old Oraibi?" Gabe asked.

Molly turned around from the front seat to look at him.

"Do you know it?" she asked.

"Well, I know of it. It's pretty famous from a cultural standpoint."

"Why is that?"

"It's generally considered to be the longest continually inhabited settlement in North America. It's believed people have lived there since around 1000 AD— almost half a century before the Europeans started showing up."

"And, when we get there you'll think that much hasn't changed since then either," Jarod said laughing.

For the next few hours the conversation seemed to lag a little. Gabe found himself dozing off a few times as the rhythmic sound of the SUV's tires humming against the pavement had almost a hypnotic effect. His brief dreams disjointed and disturbing, and when he would startle awake from the few brief moments of sleep he was left with the gnawing feeling that Molly may never see her brother alive again. He wondered if she was having the same feeling. If so, she was giving it no credence by acknowledging it out loud.

They stopped at truck stop on Interstate 40 just

outside of Winslow, Arizona to gas up the Range Rover, and to grab some food.

"I know gas station pizza doesn't make the best dinner," Jarod said. "But, it's a lot better than anything we'll find once we're off the main road."

After leaving the truck stop, they headed north up state route 87 and into the Navajo Reservation. While still a paved road, the direct route into the Indian country had reduced to two narrow lanes. Gabe noticed a distinct reduction in the amount of commercial activity, and scant little traffic other than themselves.

The Hopi Reservation is comprised of over a little more than twenty five hundred square miles, and is completely encompassed by the Navajo reservation which surrounds it. The reservation was established in 1882 by the executive order of President Chester A. Arthur. While its location kept white settlers from encroaching on Hopi land, it did not protect them from their ancient rivals—the Navajo. As late as the 1970s the two tribes were still squabbling over land rights.

The term *Hopi* was a shortened version of what the people called themselves—*Hopituh Shi-nu-mu*. Roughly translated from their native language, the term means *the peaceful people*. The first recorded European contact with the Hopi was by the Spanish in 1540. At the time, the Spanish explorers estimated that there were around sixteen thousand members of the tribe living in the area. Today, the census counts the Hopi population at fewer than seven thousand.

They had been driving on the Navajo land for about forty five minutes before they reached the border of the Hopi Reservation. Based on the way Jarod had described the relationship between the Hopi and the Navajo, Gabe had expected a more substantial border. However, only a road sign noted that they had left the Navajo Nation and had entered Hopi land.

It was nearly 8:30 when Jarod pulled the SUV up to the tribal headquarters in the small village of Kykotsmovi, Arizona. Gabe noticed that night had fallen, except for the slightest bit of orange still visible in the far Western sky.

"We need to check-in with the tribal office," Jarod said exited the car. "It's required for all visitors to the reservation."

Mike Sinquah was more than a little annoyed that he had been required to work so late all week. At other times, he might find the quietness of the office in the evening useful for studying or reading, but tonight he found himself only wanting to leave and go home.

Normally, the Hopi tribal office was only open until around five o'clock or so. However, for the past few days the tribal council had required that it stay open until Mike received a call from one of the elders saying it was OK to close down for the night. Last night, that call did not come until almost midnight.

He had no idea why the sudden change in policy, and knew it would do him no good to ask. They had given him some vague instructions on what to do with visitors, but it had not made a lot of sense to him. The tribal council would do as they see fit, and it was not up to him to question their authority or wisdom. So, for the third night in the row, he sat alone in the tribal office.

He was just contemplating turning on the television for a little background noise, when he was startled by the sound of the door to the office being opened. The small set of wind chimes connected to the inside of the door made a faint tinkling sound as the door opened and a tall white man entered.

"Good evening," the visitor said politely. "My name is Jarod McIntire."

He had briefly considered adding the title agent to his name, but then reconsidered it at the last second. He had found that people sometimes react strangely when told they are being visited by an agent from the FBI. In this case, he felt it best to keep a low profile.

"Good evening," the young Native American man said in return. "I'm sorry, but all of the tribal elders are gone for the night, so if you've come to talk with one of them you'll have to come back tomorrow."

"Actually, I'm visiting the reservation with two of my colleagues. We've come here to consult with Betty Honantewa on a professional matter. Do you know her?"

Mike Sinquah looked at the visitor as if he had just said one of the stupidest things he had ever heard.

"Of course I know Betty Honantewa. Every Hopi does. And, for that matter—I'd guess most of the Navajo too."

Jarod nodded. He realized after asking the question that it must have sounded very foolish. Betty Honantewa was considered a hero, not only to the Hopi but most of the other Native American tribes as well.

"Of course, I'm sure you do—I apologize. It would be hard not to know of someone of her stature."

The young man nodded, the brief flare of indignation he had felt a few seconds ago quickly fading. Jarod sensed that he had made the appropriate amends.

"I wanted to register our group with the tribal office as required."

Mike Sinquah nodded and pulled out a large book used for registering visitors to the reservation. He opened the book to the current page, and turned the volume around so that it would face the visitor. He handed him a pen.

Jarod registered himself, Molly and Gabe. Not knowing an address for the other two, he decided to just use the address of the bureau field office in Phoenix. He had started to contemplate earlier in the evening that no one besides the three of them knew where they were or what they were doing. Molly had refused to call Vickie and fill her in, since she was worried about upsetting her this close to when the baby is due. It would not be much of a trail, but if he listed the FBI field office it could at least alert someone that they had been here. Just in case…

"How long will you be staying on the reservation?" the young man asked, startling Jarod from his thoughts.

"Just a few hours, probably. I imagine we'll find a hotel tonight near Tuba City."

The young man nodded at him again, and retrieved his registration book.

"Do you need directions to Betty's?"

"I don't think so. We just keep heading down this road and it leads straight into Old Oraibi, right?"

"Yes, that's right. It's only a few miles down the road to Betty's place."

"Well, thanks for your help. You have a good night."

"You too, sir," Mike Sinquah said smiling.

The young man waited until the visitor had walked out the door to the tribal office and closed it firmly behind him. He waited for another few seconds just to make sure the man did not immediately return for some reason. He then picked up the phone and dialed a number from memory.

"They finally showed up," he said nearly immediately to the person who answered. "Yes, they're heading exactly where you said they would go."

He paused for a moment and listened to the response. This was apparently very welcome news to the voice on the other end of the line. Mike Sinquah took it as welcome news as well.

"Does that mean I can finally get out of here for the night?"

He was only out of the car for less than five minutes, when he returned and opened the driver's door.

"That didn't take very long," Molly said.

"Yeah. It's not like there was a line of people waiting to register with the tribal office this time of the evening."

Neither Gabe or Molly said anything in response. The entire village looked utterly deserted, so it was not a surprise to either one. In fact, Gabe was surprised that there had been anyone in the office at all. Jarod restarted the Range Rover's engine and continued down the dusty road. Within a few minutes they had entered the outskirts of Old Oraibi.

Gabe had been on a few Indian reservations while researching indigenous art. His experience so far had shown that while the reservations were definitely unique and distinct from the rest of the country, elements of modern American society always had some encroachment. Whether that be the many mobile home communities, or a Coca-Cola machine at any of the hundreds of arts and crafts stores catering to the tourists. Old Oraibi, however, was different.

If he had not have been riding in a modern automobile, he might have been convinced that he had entered a world hundreds of years in the past. Pueblo dwellings that looked as if they had been there for centuries were etched into the sides of the mesa. Even dwellings that Gabe assumed must be newer were built in the same ancient style. Old Oraibi seemed somehow completely untouched by the modern world which existed outside the reservation.

While the buildings in the village lacked any real addresses, Jarod had learned of the approximate location of Betty Honantewa's home from his friend in the state police. He parked the car on the dirt road right outside of the home which most closely matched the description he was given. He killed the engine, and the three quietly got out of the car.

Just then, the door to the house opened and an older woman walked out toward them. She looked directly at Molly.

"I assume you've come searching for your brother," she said.

CHAPTER 25

Old Oraibi, Arizona (Current Day)

Molly was surprised by the greeting from the old woman.

"You know where my brother Mark went?" she asked.

"I know where he was *going*," the woman said. "Where he *went* may be another story entirely."

Gabe could sense Molly's frustration. She was not in any mood for riddles.

"Please excuse us ma'am," Gabe said. "Are you professor Honantewa?"

The old woman laughed.

"I haven't been called *professor* Honantewa since the tyrant Reagan was in office."

Gabe smiled nervously. This woman was certainly going to live up to her reputation.

"How did you know Mark was my brother?" Molly asked.

"There will be plenty of time to answer all of your questions," Betty Honantewa said, holding her door open wider. "But right now why don't the three of you come in and relax a little bit. You have to be exhausted from the trip."

Betty Honantewa had a full meal prepared that was more than enough for all four of them. Since she clearly lived alone in the small house, it was almost like she had been expecting them.

Molly immediately started asking her questions about Mark, but Betty politely—but firmly—refused to discuss it until after the meal. Gabe could sense Molly's frustration, but also realized that she understood she had no alternative but to acquiesce to their host's wishes.

Gabe was feeling more than a little ashamed for having eaten two dinners, but the old Native American woman's food was so good he had a difficult time maintaining the guilt. Plus, the pizza from the interstate gas station should hardly count.

After dinner, Betty Honantewa cleared away the dishes, and returned with a hot pot of a very thick and rich coffee. She poured a cup for each of her guests, but Gabe noticed that she declined to partake herself.

"When you get old like me, you find that caffeine after noon will keep you up all night," she said, almost as if she had read Gabe's mind.

Gabe smiled and nodded, but said nothing.

"Ma'am," Molly said. "I really have tried to be patient, but I'm really worried about my brother."

"Of course, child. I just wanted you to be fed and rested before we started such a talk."

"You said you knew where Mark was going?"

"Yes, unfortunately I do. Despite my best attempts to talk him out of it."

"Professor Honantewa," Gabe said. "From information we've been able to piece together, we believe Mark was headed toward an area of the canyon called the Temple of Isis. Is that correct?"

"It is correct in that it is the white man's name for it. My people call it *sipapu*."

"Sipapu?" Gabe asked.

"In Hopi mythology, it is the place where the human race emerged from inside the depths of the Earth to occupy the world."

"What do you mean?" Molly asked.

"Like most cultures, my people have a story that

explains how all of humankind came to be. We believe that all life originated from below the Earth, and that a great schism between the people caused one group of people—the Hopi—to leave the underground world and live upon the surface. The others—called the *Hisatinom*—stayed in the underground world."

Gabe nodded, but said nothing. As part of his research into the art of the Native Americans, he was familiar with the Hopi legend of creation.

"My people believe that there are actually four worlds; only one of which is the surface. The other three exist in multiple levels below the Earth. That is why your brother came to see me. He wanted my perspective—both as a Hopi and as an academic—on these legends. He was also very interested in the parallels between the legends of my people and the Sumerians."

"The Sumerians?" Gabe asked.

"Yes, there are many similarities between the legends of the Hopi and those of the ancient Sumerians. For instance, both cultures believe the creating father's name is KA, but both believe man was created by a woman. There are many, many similarities between the cultures—both in vocabulary and mythology."

"There are also many parallels between the Sumerians and the Christian Bible," Gabe said.

"Yes, we discussed that as well. He told me he believed that he could prove the theory of cultural diffusionism by what he expected he would find in the canyon."

"And, what did you think?"

"I think that there are many mysteries that humans will never really understand. But, I believe that his theories definitely fit within the realm of the mythology of my ancestors."

"So," Molly said. "You believe that there are actually people living in other worlds located below the Grand Canyon?"

"What I believe is a complex tapestry. However, I do not believe the story my people have of our creation is any more unbelievable than that of an all powerful deity creating the entire universe in six days."

Molly had to privately admit that the old Indian woman had a good point with that one.

"Have you ever been to this place called sipapu?" Jarod asked.

"No, I never have. My people regard it as a sacred— but dangerous place."

"Dangerous? Why?" Molly asked.

"It represents the exact spot where the original people split, and chose two different paths. It represents all that is known—and unknown about the universe. My grandfather told stories about people who would go out in search of sipapu—only to never return."

"It doesn't help that it's located in one of the most brutal places on Earth," Jarod said.

Betty Honantewa smiled at him widely.

"Yes, young man, you've got an excellent point about that."

She turned and looked toward Molly, her smile disappearing.

"That is the real reason I discouraged your brother from this expedition. I may be a lot of things, but I'm a pragmatic old woman. I was much more concerned about the physical difficulties of the place than any mystical dangers."

"But," Molly said. "He wouldn't listen to you, right?" Molly could sympathize with the woman; Mark had often reacted to her advice the same way.

"No, I'm afraid not. I begged for him to let my nephew accompany him. He's an experienced river guide, and probably knows the canyon better than anyone I know. But, he was out on a river tour and wouldn't be back for three days. Mark said he couldn't wait—his rafting permit was scheduled to expire too soon to wait for Danny to guide him."

Betty noticed that her guests had all finished their coffee, and she walked to the stove to bring the pot back for refills. Both Gabe and Jarod took her up on the offer; Molly politely declined any more of the strong coffee.

"I assume I won't be able to talk the three of you out of attempting the trip either, will I?"

"No ma'am," Molly said. "There's still a chance we can find Mark, and there's no way that I can give up that chance."

Betty nodded. She had known the answer to the question before asking it.

"My nephew Danny has now returned. I assume you'll at least allow him to accompany you?"

"Of course, ma'am," Gabe said. "We have secured a river permit ourselves so we're ready to leave first thing in the morning."

"I'm not even going ask how you managed to secure a river permit on the spur of the moment like that."

"That's probably wise, ma'am," Gabe said smiling.

"Well, we'd better get some rest if we're setting off at the crack of dawn tomorrow," Jarod said, yawning. "There's still a few motels near Tuba City?"

"Yes, but you won't need them. I insist you three spend the night with me. It's not the Ritz—but it's comfortable."

"Thank you very much," Molly said. "We appreciate your hospitality—and help."

"There's one other thing you should know," Betty

said walking to an old roll top desk in the corner. "He left these with me. He was afraid of losing them in the river, and I think he had a feeling someone might come looking for him if things didn't work out for the best."

Jarod was immediately reminded of the thoughts that had worried him in the tribal office. He understood Mark had experienced the same feelings he had—*just in case...*

She handed several bound books to Gabe. One was a notebook that contained research notes from Mark. But, it was the four other volumes that most interested Gabe. He looked at the embossed cover of the first leather-bound volume. It said:

Personal Journal of Miss Julia Morgan

CHAPTER 26

Old Oraibi, Arizona (Current Day)

G abe knew that he needed to get some sleep to be ready for the journey through the canyon tomorrow, but he found it nearly impossible to stop reading Julia Morgan's journals.

He started with the oldest book whose first entry was dated January, 1880 when Julia Morgan was eight years old. The journal had been a Christmas gift to her from her father, and in her first entry she pledged to write in it every day. The young girl had fulfilled her commitment for several months, but Gabe noticed that after that the entries became less frequent.

Most of the early entries were the typical musings that Gabe would have expected from a young girl, but at a certain point (Gabe calculated that it must have been when Julia was around eleven or twelve) the tone of the journal

writings changed. The first entry that Gabe noticed was from
June of 1883.

> *June 7, 1883*
> *I no longer believe that the dreams that I am*
> *experiencing are dreams in the normal sense. Obviously,*
> *they are dreams because I'm asleep when they occur. But, it*
> *doesn't make sense that I would have the exact same dream*
> *almost every night. At first—right after we returned from the*
> *canyon—I couldn't remember much (if anything) of them. But*
> *over the last several months I find I can remember more and*
> *more. I feel like I should tell mother and father, but I do not*
> *want to alarm them. I should understand more before I talk*
> *about it to anyone. Even father.*

Gabe was impressed with how adult Julia's thoughts
and writing seemed to be in this entry. Others from the
previous months had seemed much more juvenile—what
he would have expected from an adolescent. But starting
with this entry, her writing seemed to take on a much more
serious tone. Subsequent entries only continued this pattern.

> *December 15, 1883*
> *I was concerned that I had lost the ability to dream*
> *about the people from the canyon, but then I remembered* the

broach that I had brought with me out of the desert. Father had known that I had it with me when the Mexican workers brought me back to the camp, but he never mentioned it after that. I remembered a few days ago that I had hidden the broach under some quilts in my cedar chest. I slept with it under my pillow last night, and once again I was able to dream about the people from the cave.

January 26, 1884

I've dreamed of the people from the canyon nearly every night since I remembered my hiding place for the broach. Although, the people call it a different name—they call it an amulet. In my dream last night they told me that I hadn't stumbled upon them, that they had sought me out for it is my destiny to help them. They have told me such wondrous things, I cannot even think of how to write them on paper. But, at the time they tell me, they make perfect sense and I understand their meaning with clarity. Their lessons are so great I cannot imagine how I could be destined to help them.

July 7, 1884

Mother believes that I have changed. I would argue the point with her, but I believe she is correct. I feel like a completely different person than I did before the people began speaking to me in my dreams. The difference between mother and I is that she is not pleased with how I have changed. However, for the first time in my life, I believe I now understand who it is to be ME.

Gabe continued to flip through the journals, and realized that was the last entry for many years that Julia Morgan mentioned the mysterious people from the canyon. Most of the entries after that were more typical journal topics for a young girl—stories about school, her interests, and even a few about boys whom she liked. Entries in later years focused on her time studying architecture, and later the building projects on which she was currently working. The next entry having anything to do with the Grand Canyon was not until the Spring of 1909.

April 25, 1909

I received a letter in the mail this morning that concerns me greatly. Actually, it was not a letter at all, but rather a clipped article from a newspaper in Arizona. The article told the story of a man who had claimed to have discovered a cave filled with Egyptian treasures hidden deep with the Grand Canyon. Obviously, I understand what this means. I have no idea who could have sent this article to me, but I know I must do something to prevent the expedition by the Smithsonian that it mentions. Perhaps I finally understand *how I may be destined to help them.*

> *May 5, 1909*
> *My meeting with Mr. Freer went extremely well.*
> *As I thought, he was more than willing to help me stop the*
> *expedition when I offered him the amulet. I realize that*
> *without the amulet I will probably no longer to be able to*
> *dream of the people from the canyon, but that is a small price*
> *to pay if I am able to protect them.*

> *August 1, 1909*
> *Oh, what have I done?*
> *Mr. Freer was able to stop the expedition by the*
> *Smithsonian, but his direct appeal to the government raised*
> *the suspicion of President Roosevelt and his military. I have*
> *recently learned from one of Mr. Hearst's reporters in Flagstaff,*
> *Arizona that the military is staging some sort of operation deep*
> *with the Grand Canyon. The reporter is perplexed as to the*
> *cause, but I am afraid I understand the object of their mission.*
> *I tried to fulfill my destiny of saving them, but I*
> *am afraid I have had the opposite impact. I fear I may have*
> *condemned them instead.*

The rest of the journals focused mostly on her work and designs; Gabe could find no other mentions of *the people from the canyon.* However, in an entry from early 1925 he recognized a sketch of the sekhmet statues he and Molly had encountered in the gardens at Hearst Castle. In the margins were a few hand scribbled notes.

> *Magnetic and luminescent substance—ZnS and Ferrite*
> *I may not be able to say what I know, but I can still tell those who can listen.*

CHAPTER 27

Arizona Desert (Current Day)

On the horizon, Gabe could see the slightest bit of orange light begin blending into the night sky. It was not quite dawn, and he was regretting having stayed awake so late reading through Julia Morgan's journals.

He, Molly, Jarod, and Betty's nephew –Danny Kasa— were driving down a deserted desert road heading into the Navajo reservation. They had loaded Jarod's Range Rover with all of the supplies they thought they would need for a minimum of five days in the canyon. Danny had explained that best case scenario, they were looking at at least two days in and two days out. Plus, however long it took them to find Mark once they arrived.

With four adults and the supplies, the Range Rover was quite crowded. As they drove in the darkness at near highway speeds, Gabe could hear the wind slapping against the four-person river raft mounted to the roof of the SUV. The raft belonged to their guide Danny, who insisted it was capable of making the trek into—and out of—the canyon. Gabe wondered how there would be enough room to include Mark on their return trip. He almost expressed that thought out loud, then thought better of it.

"So, Danny," Jarod asked, interrupting Gabe's thoughts. "Where do you expect us to enter the Colorado?"

"Actually, we're going to start out in the Little Colorado," Danny replied. "We can follow it until it merges with the Colorado at the edge of the canyon."

"Is that the fastest route?" Molly asked.

"Yeah, most definitely. There are only certain places where you can actually enter the Colorado, and all of those would be at least a full day's drive. Plus, they're clogged with tourists. Trust me, this is the best—and fastest—option."

Molly nodded, but still seemed skeptical. Gabe could sense her frustration, but knew they had no option but to trust their guide.

"Where are you planning for us to enter the Little Colorado, then?" Jarod asked as a follow up to his original question.

"There's a pretty good entry point near Cameron. It's still in the Navajo reservation, but there won't be any traffic."

"How long will we be in the river?" Molly asked.

"The actual term is *on the river*," Danny replied. "And, that will be a full two days. It's not an easy trip."

"And this is really the fastest way to get to the Temple of Isis?"

"Yes, ma'am—it is." Danny paused for a moment then added, "My aunt said you'd keep me honest."

Gabe smiled. He noticed Molly did not.

"Will the river be really rough this time of year?" Gabe asked.

"It's going to be a mixed bag. The full route should be navigable since it's still technically the rainy season. Of course, that also means there'll be a lot of water flowing through the rapids too."

Gabe did not like the sound of that prediction. He had never been white water rafting before in his life, and he imagined this was far from a beginner's route. But, he would do anything necessary to help Molly find her brother.

"My aunt says that you have the river permits? We won't see many people for the first day, but after that we're going to catch up with the tourists. The park personnel will need to see the permits."

"Don't worry," Gabe said. "We have the permits we need."

He declined to mention that they had been personally signed by the Secretary of the Interior.

They reached the village of Cameron a little after six in the morning. By the time they were on the outskirts of town, the night had finally faded into the brightness of the dawn. Cameron was a small Navajo town with a population of less than one thousand. Its main claim to fame was that it was the home of a large trading post of Native American crafts. It was popular with tourists seeking the "real" Indian experience.

After passing through Cameron, which really consisted of nothing more than a few mobile home parks and the trading post, Danny Kasa instructed Jarod to make a left turn onto a narrow dirt road.

"You might want to make sure your four wheel drive is engaged," Danny said.

Jarod nodded, and reached down and pressed a button on the center panel near the gear shift mechanism. Nearly immediately after turning onto the road, Jarod hit a large pothole which jared the contents and occupants of the SUV.

"How long is the road going to be like this?" Jarod asked.

"It's only going to be a few miles, but I'm sure it's going to feel like a lot longer."

Looking around, all Gabe could see was desolate desert in every direction. It was hard to even tell in some areas where the desert ended and the road began. Jarod was driving less than twenty miles per hour, but the Range Rover was still bouncing violently. Gabe fought the feelings of car sickness which was quickly rushing over him.

At just the point where Gabe was sure he was going to have to tell Jarod to stop the SUV so he could vomit, Danny Kasa had told him to pull off to the side and stop.

"This is as far as we can get in the car," Danny said. "We need to hike over in that direction."

"Are we going to have to carry all this stuff with us?" Molly asked.

"Unfortunately, yes. But, it's less than a quarter mile."

They got out of the SUV and each put on a large backpack loaded with necessary supplies. They untied the raft from the top of Range Rover, and each grabbed a corner.

"The worst part is going to be carrying the raft. But, we'll be in the water soon."

Even though the walk would have been less than a quarter mile as Danny promised, they all soon found themselves exhausted from the load they were carrying.

"Let's stop for a minute and rest," Jarod said.

They dropped the raft and the backpacks each were carrying, and sat down on the desert sand. Gabe could not believe it could feel this hot so early on an April morning. He stood up and looked into the distance.

"Where exactly are we headed?" Gabe asked.

"Just down that bank is a small tributary that will lead us directly into the Little Colorado," Danny said.

Gabe began walking in the direction Danny had pointed. He thought if he could see exactly how far the riverbank was now, it would seem more manageable when they were lugging all of the supplies.

As he got closer to the bank, he noticed that the ground had gotten considerably more wet, and his boots began to sink into the wet sand. He was trying to pull his feet out to walk back toward the others when he noticed Jarod and Danny walking up behind him. Danny put out his arm to stop Jarod from moving closer.

"Hey," Gabe said with a nervous laugh. "The ground seems a little soggy here."

Gabe was surprised at how deeply—and how quickly—he was sinking into the wet sand.

"Gabe, try not to struggle too much," Danny said, purposely keeping his tone low and calm. "I need you to do exactly what I tell you."

Despite Danny's obvious attempt to keep him calm, Gabe found himself beginning to panic.

"Why? What's wrong?"

"You've wandered into some quicksand."

Quicksand! Gabe felt the full force of the panic wash over him.

CHAPTER 28

Washington DC (Current Day)

Reginald Allard looked up from his desk to his assistant who had just entered his office. It was late in the evening—much later than he was accustomed to working. Although, he supposed this thing must be expected of a member of the President's cabinet. However, tonight he was still sitting in his office by his own choosing.

"Excuse me, Mr. Secretary. The call you were expecting is on the line."

He briefly acknowledged her with a slight nod. It was subtle, but she understood his meaning perfectly. She was a holdover appointment from his predecessor, and he had been impressed with her so far. While it would normally be his style to completely clean house and bring in his own people, this time he had decided to take a different approach.

He thought it might be helpful to have someone around who knew the ropes. Especially if that person felt a loyalty to him.

Reginald Allard had discovered a long time ago that nothing inspired loyalty like not firing someone when they were clearly expecting you to do the opposite.

The assistant left the office, and closed the door firmly behind her. Allard picked up the phone receiver and pressed the flashing button.

"This is Secretary Allard."

"Mr. Secretary," the voice on the other side of the line said hesitantly. "This is Chief Abigail Walters of the US Parks Police."

"Chief Walters," Allard said pleasantly. "Thank you so much for taking the time to call me."

He was trying his hardest to sound sincere, but he knew that the woman really had no other choice. Who would refuse a call to a man who was not only her boss's boss, but also reported directly to the President of the United States?

"Of course, sir. Although, I have to admit—I actually accused my assistant of getting the message wrong."

Allard laughed. The woman was attempting to charm him. And, she was not doing a half-bad job at it.

"Well, you can apologize to your assistant. She got the message correct—the Secretary of the Interior needs your help and advice."

"Of course, sir. Anyway at all I can help you, sir."

Allard smiled again. He loved working with uniformed personnel. He loved the formality of their approach to him; the way they would treat him with unquestioned respect. One of the few things he had actually enjoyed about being governor was the contingent of state police officers who would travel with him at all times.

He found Abigail Walters to be just as proud and respectful as his officers from Indiana. Before contacting the chief of the Parks Police he had done some research on this woman. She was a twenty-eight year veteran of the force, working her way up from a beat cop at the Statue of Liberty all the way to Chief of US Parks Police.

The woman's reputation was beyond reproach, having received more commendations over her career than he could count. Allard had been impressed with what he had read; she was an impressive representative of an impressive organization. During his research, he had been surprised to read the US Parks Police was actually the oldest uniformed federal law enforcement agency in the United States. It had been personally founded in 1791 by George Washington.

"I certainly appreciate that, Chief Walters. I'm looking for some information on an area in the Grand Canyon."

"The canyon, sir?"

"Yes. Specifically, an area of the canyon named the Temple of Isis."

There was silence on the other end of the line. For a moment, he thought their call may have been disconnected. Then, he heard the woman swallow harder than she probably had intended.

"Yes, sir. I see, sir."

"Are you aware of the area I'm talking about?"

"Yes, sir," she said slowly. "That's a very remote area of the canyon. The Parks Service classifies it as sector nine."

"Sector nine?"

"Yes, sir. Most of the national parks are divided into different sectors for patrol purposes and reporting. That area of the Grand Canyon is part of a region called sector nine."

"Well, then captain—what can you tell me about sector nine?"

"Unfortunately, very little. It's actually in a restricted area of the canyon"

"Restricted?" Allard said with a surprised lilt in his voice. "You're the captain of the US Parks Police—it seems unusual that any area of a national park could be off limits to you."

"Yes, I understand that it sounds unusual. In fact, it's the only park where such a situation exists."

"Why is the area off limits?"

"I honestly don't know, sir. The only information I've been given is that it's in a Federally restricted area and that its off limits to everyone—even the US Parks Service."

"Whose jurisdiction does sector nine fall under, then?"

"Honestly, sir—I don't know," she said. She paused for a moment as if she was internally debating whether or not to continue. Ultimately she decided to trust her instincts and finish her thought. "But if I were a betting woman, I'd put my money on one of the intelligence organizations—probably either the CIA or NSA. This thing has their fingerprints all over it."

Allard exhaled deeply. This was not the story he had expected to hear when he had asked the police captain to call him. But, this information would still be extremely valuable to him.

"Well thank you, Captain Walters for being so candid with me. I certainly appreciate your insight."

"Of course, Mr. Secretary. I only wish I could have had more information I could have given you, sir."

"You have helped me quite a bit, actually. Thank you."

Allard then hung up the phone and buzzed the intercom for his assistant. She entered the office a few seconds later.

"Yes, Mr. Secretary?"

"Margo, I need you to contact the White House for me. I need to go up there tonight and have a talk."

"You need to see the President this late, Mr. Secretary?"

"No," Allard said. "I need to see his chief-of-staff."

CHAPTER 29

Arizona Desert (Current Day)

"Gabe," Danny said quietly. "I need you to stay calm."

"Calm? I'm stuck in fucking quicksand!" Gabe said, his voice rising into what was quickly approaching a scream.

"It's going to be OK. Jarod and I can get you out. Now, stop struggling!"

The sharp tone of Danny's command seemed to snap Gabe out of his panic. He heard him instruct Jarod to go find some sort of tree limb or other sturdy stick. He felt almost frozen as he watched Jarod scurry off into the desert.

"That's good, Gabe," Danny said. "Just try not to move too much. We'll have you out of there in no time."

Although only few minutes, it seemed like it took hours for Jarod to return. He came back to Danny carrying two large limbs that were each about four feet in length.

"Yeah, this should work," Danny said in reply.

He threw the limb toward Gabe and it landed just behind his head, perpendicular to his body.

"Gabe, I want you to put your arms backward over the limb and lean back. Roll your back over the top of the wood."

As Gabe leaned back it changed his center of balance, and he realized his legs were beginning to rise. Within a few seconds, he was actually floating on his back on top of the quicksand.

"That's great," Danny said. "Now, just continue to roll backward on the limb."

As he rolled backward he felt the ground begin to firm up around him. Within a few seconds, he felt Jarod and Danny grabbing him at either arm and pulling him to his feet. He slipped freely from the wet sandy prison.

"There you go," Danny said laughing and clearly relieved.

Gabe looked at Jarod who was still holding his arm, and looked practically nauseated with concern.

"Are you ok?" he asked.

"Yeah, a little shook up. A little sandy too, I guess. Like a bad day at the beach."

Jarod smiled, and Gabe felt touched by his genuine

concern.

They turned around and walked back toward where Molly was still resting with all of their gear.

"What took you guys so long?" she asked as they approached. "And why the hell are you so wet?"

Gabe gave Molly the bare minimum details about his experience with the quicksand. There was no sense in reminding her further of all the dangers Mark had faced out here alone. They picked up their gear and the raft and headed down the bank toward the stream. They gave the area of quicksand a wide berth as they passed.

They walked down the steep bank each carrying a corner of the raft. Danny led them into the edge of the stream. He pulled the paddles out of one of the bags and handed them each an oar. Gabe was shocked by how freezing cold the water felt. This was not going to be an easy trip.

Danny instructed the other three to get into the raft, then he gave it a hard shove and pushed the raft into the current. He ran through the shallow water and jumped in himself just before the current caught the raft and started propelling it downstream.

"Well, we're on our way," he said, settling into his seat

in the raft. "It's about fifty one miles until we meet up with the Colorado River in the canyon."

"How long will that take—a few hours?" Molly asked.

Danny laughed loudly.

"This isn't a car on a paved highway. We'll be lucky if we make it there within eighteen hours. The good news is that it's still the rainy season, so at least the whole route should be navigable."

"Eighteen hours just to get into the canyon? I can't believe this is the fastest way we can get there!"

"Well, ma'am, I'm more than welcome to listen to any ideas you have. But, I've rafted through this canyon more times than I can count, so you may just want to trust my experience on this."

Gabe could tell that Danny's patience with Molly's constant questioning of him was fading quickly. Molly seemed to pick up on that too.

"I'm sorry. I'm just really worried about my brother, and I'm afraid it's making me act like a real bitch."

"No problem, ma'am—I understand. You have my word I'll do everything I can to help you find him."

The reached the Little Colorado River a few hours later, and the river became significantly wider and deeper than the lesser tributary where they had started. Around noon they landed the boat on a wide sandy area on the river's edge and ate some sandwiches they had packed to bring along on the trip.

The next several hours were relatively uneventful. They encountered a few small rapids that Danny said would be nothing compared to what they would face later in the canyon. They spent the entire day on the river and never saw another person aside from themselves. Gabe could not imagine making this trip alone like Mark had done.

Around five o'clock in the afternoon, Gabe noticed that the sun had sunk considerably lower in the sky and was slipping behind the many rocky hills which lined the river.

"We're a few miles from where I think we should camp for the night," Danny said. "It's a nice flat area in a bend in the river. In fact, it's called Devil's Bend."

"Sounds like a great place to spend a dark night in the wilderness," Gabe said.

"Yeah, the name doesn't really do it justice. It's a great place to camp for the night—it's dry and safe. Well, as safe as you can get in the middle of the desert at night, I guess."

Gabe realized right then that a good night's sleep out here was going to be unlikely. Regardless of how safe Danny Kasa proclaimed it to be.

They reached Devil's Bend just before six in the evening. By that time, the sun had pretty much all together disappeared behind the hills which surrounded them. They pulled the raft up onto the sandy bank far enough so that there was no danger of the river catching it accidentally. They unloaded their bags from the raft and carried them further up the bank.

"We should be able to find some firewood over in the brush at the edges of the hill," Danny said, pointing to the hillside.

Gabe and Jarod took that as their cue to so look for some wood, and returned a few minutes later with enough fuel to start a good fire. Danny arranged the wood in a pyre, and lit it with some waterproof matches from one of the packs.

In the distance, Gabe could hear a coyote—or some other animal of the night—howl mournfully.

Yes, sleep was going to be very elusive tonight.

CHAPTER 30

Devils Bend, Arizona (Current Day)

After working off the stiffness from sitting in the boat all day, and eating some dinner, Gabe felt significantly better than he had when they first landed at Devil's Bend. He, Molly, Jarod and Danny Kasa sat around the roaring fire. If he could forget for a moment why they were out here, it could almost be an enjoyable evening.

Everyone else seemed a little more relaxed now too—even Molly. Danny was telling tales of his exploits bringing tourists up and down the river, and they were enjoying the funny stories. Gabe looked across the fire and saw the orange glow reflecting off Jarod's face, who was laughing at one of the tales. Gabe would have found it hard to believe, but he actually looked even more handsome in this light.

The group laughter from Danny's most recent story

was fading, and Gabe could clearly hear the night sounds of the desert, along with the crackling of the fire. He noticed Molly had become very quiet over the last several minutes.

"You know what I can't understand?" Molly asked, but did not wait for anyone to reply. "I don't understand why Mark would want to risk his life just to prove that ancient Egyptians had been in America. It seems like a silly thing to care so much about."

"Maybe," Gabe said. "But, the true essence of science—and art—is the pursuit of truth. I think that's really what Mark is seeking—an understanding of the truth."

Molly nodded, but she still looked unconvinced.

"My people believe that sipapu is a very sacred place," Danny said. "The place where the cave dwellers emerged was the cradle of life on Earth."

"From what I've read in Julia Morgan's journals, it appears she felt the same way," Gabe said. "I don't know exactly what happened to her out in the canyon when she was a little girl, but it certainly had a profound impact on her life."

"That's what I don't understand," Jarod said.

Gabe looked at him questioningly.

"Why all the mystery? Why leave all the clues? She worked for one of the most powerful media barons in history—she could have gotten the story of what was in the canyon published in every paper from coast to coast."

"From her journals, I can only tell that she felt very protective of what she experienced in the canyon," Gabe said. "But, on the other hand it goes back to what I said about truth being the essence of art and science. She couldn't bear for the truth to be lost—but yet she couldn't directly tell it herself. She tried to leave a path for others to follow instead."

Jarod nodded at Gabe's explanation.

"Well, boys," Molly said, rising from in front of the fire. "This conversation is getting a little philosophical for me. I'm hitting the hay."

"I think that's an excellent idea," Danny said, also rising. "We've got another long day on the river tomorrow—and it's best to be well rested when you face the river."

Danny Kasa and Molly both began walking toward their tents. As she passed, Molly briefly put her hand on Jarod's shoulder.

"Looks like she is finally warming up to you," Gabe said after Molly was out of earshot.

"Yeah, looks like it. Maybe she won't treat me like the world's biggest prick after we get back in the office. Is she always this hard to win over?"

Gabe laughed.

"Yeah, I guess she usually is."

"I'm not even sure what I did to make her dislike me so much. What did she tell you about me?"

"The truth?"

"Of course, that's why I'm asking."

"She referred to you as an uptight closet case who only got your position in the bureau because of your father."

Then it was Jarod's turn to laugh.

"Well, I'm glad you didn't hold anything back. The funny part is that if she knew my father, she'd know him helping me get a position with the bureau would be the last thing he'd do."

"Why? Who is your father?"

"Randolph McIntire."

"*The* Randolph McIntire—the four term senator from Arizona?"

"Yep, that would be him. He wanted me to be an attorney then go into the family business—politics."

"And, you rebelled?" Gabe asked.

"Yeah, I guess you can say that. I graduated from law school and the next day I enrolled at the state police academy. The old man wouldn't talk to me for months," Jarod said. "Of course, that didn't stop him from using me as part of his 'tough on crime' stance during his next campaign."

"So…what about the other part?"

"What? The closet case comment?"

Gabe shrugged, a little embarrassed.

"Well, I guess I am who I am. Yeah, maybe I'm not

real open about my personal life with people at work. But, I'd hardly call myself a closet case."

"Well that's good. Considering J. Edgar Hoover's proclivities, I'd like to think the FBI would be a little more open."

"Yeah," Jarod said laughing. "I'm not sure that's exactly the case."

They sat there without speaking for the next few minutes, watching the fire begin to dwindle down.

"So, what about you?" Jarod asked.

"Me?"

"Yeah. You said you thought Molly was warming up to me. What about you?"

Again, Gabe looked a little embarrassed.

"I think I started warming up to you after about the first five minutes."

Jarod laughed. Gabe could not tell in the light of the fire, but he thought Jarod might be blushing as well.

"I think Molly and Danny had the right idea," Jarod said. "It's late, and I need to get some sleep."

Jarod stood up and began walking to his tent. Right before he got to the opening of the tent, he turned to look back toward Gabe.

"Yeah, I guess I warmed up to you pretty quick too," Jarod said. Then, without another word he turned and entered his tent.

Despite being in the middle of the desert in the dark cool night, and the seriousness of their mission—Gabe felt very happy in that moment.

CHAPTER 31

Little Colorado River, Arizona (Current Day)

Once again, the four were up and awake before the break of dawn.

They ate a quick breakfast of protein bars, then packed up the gear and reloaded it back onto the raft. By the time the light had established itself enough so that they could safely see, they were ready to set out again on the river.

Within an hour of leaving Devil's Bend, they reached the confluence of the Little Colorado and the Colorado rivers. The mix of colors from the two rivers joining was striking; with the Little Colorado being a muddled brown from the runoff of recent rains, and the Colorado being a vibrant emerald green.

As the raft entered it was quickly swept into the quick flowing current of the Colorado.

"Paddle into the direction of the current," Danny yelled to his passengers above the roar of the river.

Within a few hundred feet of their entry into the Colorado River—and simultaneously, the Grand Canyon—the waters calmed significantly.

"Lady and gentleman," Danny said with mock dramatic flair. "We have entered the Grand Canyon."

Gabe looked up at the sights surrounding him. The sheer canyon cliffs on either side of them climbed so high, he could not actually see the tops of them. The colors in the exposed layers of rock were beautiful and vibrant; each strata representing hundreds of thousands of years in time. Gabe realized that about six million years worth of the Earth's history was stretched out before and above him right now.

"It's absolutely beautiful," he said to no one in particular.

"Enjoy the scenery while you can. It's beautiful and calm right now," Danny said. "But that will change soon enough."

About five miles after entering the canyon they encountered the first white water of any note in an area called Lava Rapids. Danny shouted instructions at them throughout the course, telling them when to paddle and on which side of the raft. Gabe was surprised at the rush of adrenalin that he got from the ride.

"That wasn't so bad," Molly said after the water had calmed again.

"Nope. But Lava is maybe a class two or three—we've got a seven or eight class coming up soon."

Gabe swallowed hard. He was not sure he was ready for that much adrenalin.

"I thought the scale only went up to a six?" he asked.

"The one through six class is the standard international scale, but for some reason the big rivers in the Western U.S. have always used a one through ten scale."

Eleven miles and a few hours later they hit the Hance Rapids, which is classified as a seven class on the Grand Canyon scale. Gabe was absolutely shocked by the ferocity and power of the river. At many points he was certain he was going to be thrown from the raft and crushed upon any of the many boulders peppered throughout their path.

He was so grateful that Betty Honantewa had insisted they make the trip with an experienced river guide. Molly said that Mark was comfortable in white water too, but he wondered how anyone could really be prepared for something like the rapids they were facing. Especially since he was rafting alone.

It seemed like it took hours for them to successfully navigate the Hance Rapids, although in reality Gabe knew it probably took no more than ten minutes or so. As the water gradually slowed to its pre-rapids calmness, he thought he could sense the relief from his fellow passengers.

"Wow," Jarod said. "Please tell me that's the worst we're going to face."

"I wish I could," Danny said. "But we still have Sockdolager coming up."

"Sockdolager?" Molly asked.

"Yeah. I guess it's an old term from the 1800s. It means *knock-out punch*."

There was a collective groan from the three passengers.

Ten miles, and about five sets of rapids later (including the infamous *Sockdolager*), they crossed below the Kaibab Bridge which links the North and South rims of the canyon. They had been on the river for nearly ten hours.

"The Bright Angel Creek campground is just up ahead—that's where we'll stop for the night," Danny announced.

Gabe fully expected Molly to argue that they should keep moving in order to get to Mark faster, but to his surprise she did not. She was soaking wet and exhausted from the day fighting the river, and actually seemed almost relieved to be getting a reprieve. Even Molly had reached her limits of toughness.

As they got closer to their evening stopping point,

they started encountering a few more tourists. Danny had told them that this was still early for the peak rafting season, but tour groups were venturing out on the river earlier and earlier every Spring. After their experiences today, Gabe was not sure he would ever want to do this again as a vacation.

They landed the raft on sandy shore, and it took the four of them to pull it up onto higher ground.

"Don't we have to worry about someone stealing the raft if we just leave it here?" Molly asked.

"No," Danny replied. "Rafters are a pretty trusting people. And, if you're out for some petty theft, you're probably not going to go to all the trouble of getting to the floor of the Grand Canyon to do it."

Gabe knew that Molly was not a trusting person by nature, especially where criminal activity was concerned. However, he suspected she was just too tired to argue the point right now. Plus, he doubted any of them felt like keeping watch over the raft all night. So, it was better to just trust their fellow tourists.

"What are those cabins over there?" Gabe asked.

"That's the Phantom Ranch," Danny replied.

"Why aren't we staying there?" Molly asked. "That looks a lot more comfortable than spending another night in a tent."

"Yeah, I wish we could. Phantom Ranch books

up months in advance—even this early in the season. But, they've got a canteen, running water, and bathrooms that we can take advantage of. So, at least it won't be quite as primitive as last night."

Almost immediately after leaving the boat to walk toward the campground office, they were approached by two officers from the Parks Service.

"Good evening folks," one of the rangers said. "We just need to check your park permits please."

Gabe reached into the waterproof fanny pack he had kept strapped to his waist since the journey began, and pulled out the permit. He handed the papers to the smiling ranger. The ranger looked at the permit; then looked directly at Gabe; then back to the permit again.

"Excuse me for a moment, sir," the ranger said.

He walked back toward where his partner had remained standing. He showed the other ranger the permit. The other ranger followed the same eye path from the permit, to Gabe, and back to the permit again. Gabe noticed the first ranger was using the radio attached to the shoulder of his uniform, and seemed to be having a rather involved conversation with someone.

"Your friend the Secretary wouldn't have fucked us over, would he?" Molly whispered into Gabe's ear.

"Oh, he's definitely the type to do so. But, I don't

think he'd risk doing that in this situation. He's got too much at risk himself."

It seemed like an eternity later, but eventually the smiling officer approached them again, and handed the permit back to Gabe.

"Thank you, sir," he said. "Everything checks out just fine. I've been told by my supervisor to let you know that you won't be approached again by any park personnel—"

He paused as if he was trying to determine what to say next. Then he added:

"*For any reason.*"

Gabe thanked the ranger, and the four continued the walk to the small wooden building which housed the campground office.

"That was a strange way to say it," Jarod said.

"Yeah," Gabe replied. "I'd say disturbingly strange."

CHAPTER 32

Grand Canyon, Arizona (Current Day)

Gabe startled awake to the sound of voices. It was the excited conversation of a group of their fellow campers who were obviously up early to continue their own journey on the river. He was not sure what time it was, but it was still dark so it had to be very early. Gabe decided that the first thing he would do when this whole thing was over was sleep for at least a week.

He stepped out of his tent and saw that Danny Kasa was already up and about, and was preparing their supplies for the day's journey. Danny looked at Gabe and nodded a greeting.

"If we can get moving as soon as it's light, we should be able to make it to the Temple of Isis by Noon."

Gabe noted that this was the first time Danny had

referred to their desired destination by its non-Hopi name.

"Do you think the water will be as rough today?" Gabe asked.

"Shouldn't be. We'll start off in Bright Angel Creek which is relatively calm, and there will be a series of smaller tributaries after that. I've actually never been that far back, but I don't anticipate a lot of white water from what I've heard."

Gabe noticed that both Molly and Jarod had emerged from their respective tents and were doing their part in preparing for the day on the river.

They pushed off into Bright Angel Creek, and Gabe was pleased to find that the water was as calm as Danny had promised. Various other streams intersected with Bright Angel at frequent intervals. Gabe noticed that Danny was paying close attention to a satellite-based GPS unit he held in his hands.

"I thought you were the expert guide?" Molly asked.

"It's hard to be an expert on a place you've never actually been," Danny said. "Don't worry—I've heard enough stories that I can get us there."

They continued rafting along for the next few hours. Every so often Danny would give the direction for them to paddle into a different tributary as they met it. This happened so often that Gabe figured by this point it would have been impossible to find their way out of here again. The fact that they were experiencing a part of the Grand Canyon most people never get to see did not hold much allure for him right now.

As their current stream meandered along, Gabe could see something in the distance. As they got closer, he realized that it was a chain link fence attached to both sides of the cliff face, and traversing the water route. The bottom of the metal fence was less than a foot above the water line.

"There's no way we're going to raft under it," Danny said. He then directed his passengers to paddle to the side to reach one of the sandy shores. They beached the raft and climbed out.

Gabe noticed that the chain link fence had a large sign mounted to the center of it. The sign read:

WARNING! RESTRICTED ACCESS—NO ENTRY
PROTECTED BAT HABITAT
U.S. PARKS SERVICE PERSONNEL ONLY
ALL TRESPASSERS WILL BE PROSECUTED

"Yeah," Molly said. "Bats my ass."

Jarod had walked away from the other three as they stood and read the sign.

"Hey you guys," he said from about ten feet away.

"Come here and look at this."

He pulled back some scrub and revealed a one man kayak that had been hidden in the vegetation.

Molly looked in the the kayak, and pulled out a yellow life preserver vest. There was a name hand written clearly on the vest. It read:

Mark Newman

Molly looked up at Gabe with a mixture of relief and hope. He noticed that there were a few tears beginning to form at the edges of her eyes.

"Well," she said. "It looks like we're heading in the right direction."

Gabe put his arm around her shoulders, and the four of them began walking back toward the chain link fence.

"It looks like we can scale the cliff near the fence," Danny said. "We can then just drop down on the other side."

The other three nodded in agreement. Gabe estimated the fence height to be around twelve feet high. Even for someone of his limited climbing experience, this should not prove to be too difficult.

"We want to limit what we carry in," Danny said. "Only the necessities—flashlights, some rope and climbing equipment, the GPS unit. And, as much water as we can carry. If—"

He stopped himself in mid-sentence, then continued.

"*When* we find Mark, he'll probably be pretty low in his water supply by now."

Danny led them over to the far edge of the fence where it had been affixed to the side of the cliff wall. He took a small grappling hook from his pack and attached it to a length of climbing rope that he pulled from the same place. He flung the grappling hook over the height of the fence. It took a few attempts, but it finally caught in the chain link on the opposite side.

He gave the rope a hard tug to ensure that it was affixed securely. He gradually began pulling himself up the rope while simultaneously using his feet to walk up the face of the cliff wall that ran perpendicular to the fence. After a few moments he reached the top of the fence. He pulled himself over the top of it so that his body was fully on the other side.

He hung onto the top of the fence and let his body hang down. He waited for a second, then let himself drop to the sandy ground below.

"We're damn lucky no one bothered to put barbed wire at the top of the fence," he said.

Danny directed the three others to follow his lead, and one-by-one each scaled the cliff wall and dropped over to the other side of the fence. At the apex of the climb, Gabe was struck by how high twelve feet could feel when looking down from that height.

After all four of them were on the opposite side of the fence, Danny retrieved the grappling hook and rope. He was hoping that there would not be a lot of rock climbing required of them for the rest of the journey, but he could not take that chance.

"How far do we walk from here?" Molly asked.

Danny studied the GPS unit for moment, then shaded his eyes and looked out at the desert land in front of them.

"I'm guessing it's about five miles—maybe a little less."

The four began walking along the narrow sandy ledge which hugged the cliff wall on one side, and the river on the other. Gabe had not brought his watch, but he looked up at the sky. From the sun's position nearly directly above them, he knew that it must be very close to noon. The four continued to walk forward; mostly in silence.

Around ninety minutes later, Danny stopped walking and pulled out the GPS unit. He looked at it, then around at the cliffs beside them.

"This should be it," Danny said quietly.

Although, Gabe sensed that he did not feel entirely

confident in that announcement.

Danny walked off the sandy ground and into the stream. Gabe had not noticed until that moment that the stream they had been following had pretty much dwindled to just a trickle at this point. Even if the chain link fence had not been blocking the creek they still would have been limited in how far the boat could have taken them.

Danny took a small pair of binoculars out of this pack and began scanning the cliffs. He noticed that several hundred feet above them was a recessed area that set back from the rest of the cliff wall.

By that point, Gabe, Molly and Jarod had joined Danny as he stood in the few inches of water that still made up the creek. The three looked up toward the area where Danny had focused his binoculars.

"There looks like there's some kind of terrace up in that area," he said pointing. "Just looks like more cliff wall though—I don't see any caverns."

Jarod motioned for Danny to hand him the binoculars, and he trained his sight on the area as well.

"Hey, that's kind of weird," Jarod said.

"What is it?"

"I can see the sun reflecting pretty heavily off of most of the cliff face, but there's an area up there that's not reflecting—it's like it's not the same kind of rock."

By this time, Gabe had taken the binoculars from Jarod, and was also staring at the area in question.

"Or, it isn't rock at all," Gabe said.

"What do you mean?" Danny asked.

"There are certain basic principles of light and reflection which this area doesn't seem to be adhering to," Gabe said, lowering the binoculars. "So, there's obviously something different about it."

"Well, that's great," Molly said. "But how are we going to get up there—that's like a thousand feet up."

Danny looked around at the brush along the side of the cliff face. Gabe noticed his eyes following a path forward and upward.

"No freakin' way," Danny said quietly.

"What?" the other three asked in near unison.

"There's a path," Danny said pointing. "It looks like it cuts back and forth quite a bit, but I think it leads up to where we want to go.

Less than thirty minutes later, they had reached the terrace they had seen from below. Gabe was pleasantly surprised at how easy the hike up from the canyon floor had been. Granted the trail had been precarious in a few places, but they had continued through without incident. Gabe amusingly thought for a moment that his car trip down the Pacific Coast Highway with Molly a few nights ago had been more treacherous than this.

Then a bad thought struck him. It had been almost *too* easy.

The ledge where the trail ended was about one hundred feet wide, and Gabe guessed about twenty feet deep as it sat back from the cliff. The area of non-reflective light which had seemed so apparent from the canyon floor was now invisible from their new vantage point facing the rock wall.

Gabe walked forward to the the cliff face, and began sweeping his hands across the cool, hard rock.

"What are you doing?" Molly asked.

"Part of this rock looked different from down below; I'm trying to see if it feels different too."

Gabe was in mid sentence when his arm suddenly disappeared up to his elbow. He heard his companions gasp loudly behind him.

He was startled for a moment, but then he realized that he had stuck his hand into a projected image. He looked around at the edges of the rock and noticed that there was a small projection device several feet off to his left that was attempting to hide in some brush. Solar collectors on the top of the device gave a strong clue as to its power source.

"Absolutely ingenious," Gabe said in what amounted to a loud whisper, more to himself than anyone.

His three companions said nothing, but continued to stare at him.

"It's some sort of holographic projection. The projector is pointing up from an angle, then reflecting down from the rock above to obscure an opening in the wall. The projection is set up so that you can be standing right in front of it and not ever really see it."

No one said anything else for what felt like several minutes. It was like they all were trying to individually reconcile what they were seeing and hearing.

Finally, Jarod spoke.

"So, I guess I was willing to think that that trail was a happy accident—or somehow naturally occurring," he said. "But I guess a high tech projector out here in the middle of the canyon confirms it. Somebody has gone to a lot of trouble to hide something pretty special up here."

Gabe noticed that Molly was flinging her pack over her shoulders and back on to her back. She pulled out a flashlight, illuminated it, then began walking forward.

"What are you doing?" Gabe asked.

"What do you think I'm doing? I'm going to find Mark."

And, with that, she was gone—seemingly vanishing through the cliff wall.

CHAPTER 33

The Temple of Isis (Current Day)

Nearly as soon as Molly had disappeared into the cliff face, the other three followed.

The first thing Gabe noticed upon entering the cavern was the absolute darkness which enveloped them. He turned back and looked at the entrance where they had just emerged. From this side the projection was a little more apparent, and the outside world looked somewhat fuzzy and muted when looking back through the optical illusion.

Even though it was dark and he could barely see anything at all, Gabe still had a sense of the enormity of the chamber they had just entered. He turned on his lantern, and his three companions did the same. All four carried high power halogen spotlights designed for professional cave explorers. Even with the combined effort of four million candle power between them, it still made barely a dent in the darkness.

Gabe directed his light at the wall just inside the entry way. The way was nearly covered with a red swastika. From the variation in design, Gabe believed it to probably be far Eastern in origin.

"What the hell," Jarod said. "Is that a Nazi swastika?"

"Actually…" Gabe began.

"Actually," Molly said interrupting. "Gabe is going to give a big lecture about how the swastika is one of the oldest symbols in history, and this one doesn't have anything to do with Nazis. Right, Gabe?"

Well, Gabe thought, *at least she listens to what I'm saying.*

"No, this is not of Nazi design. It resembles ones I've seen documented in Indian texts. It's a very old design—maybe fourth or fifth century B.C."

Danny Kasa pulled the satellite GPS unit from his pack and pressed several buttons. He noticed that the others were watching him closely.

"I'm marking the location of the entrance on the GPS so we can find our way back out," he explained.

"Will we still have a satellite signal when we get deeper into the cave?" Jarod asked.

"I'm not sure. But, I figure it's a worth a shot."

The four turned in the opposite direction of the projection obscured entrance and began walking deeper into the cavern.

After a few hours of journeying deeper into the caves, Gabe found that his vision was gradually growing more accustomed to the darkness. He was unsure of the actual size of this underground world, but knew it as absolutely huge. Gabe had been able to discern that they had walked into at least four distinct chambers since entering the complex.

It was in the third chamber where they had encountered the first treasure.

Gabe actually thought the term *treasure* may be significantly underestimating what they had found. When they encountered the first life size gold statues, Gabe nearly dropped his flashlight. He thought they had walked into a group of people standing in the darkness.

Closer inspection proved the figures to be not humans at all, but rather life size gold statues. Gabe directed his light along the height of of one of the statues, and was amazed at what he saw. He estimated the figure to be several thousands of years old—if not even older.

"Christ," Molly said in amazement. "Are these things

made out of gold?"

"It certainly looks that way," Gabe said. "And I'm guessing they're very, very old."

Gabe pulled his cell phone out of his pocket and used its camera to take a photo of the gold figures. In the split second when the flash fired, he could see in his peripheral vision that there many other items in this chamber. His initial thought was that it could take a museum staff months to catalog all of the objects hidden here.

"What are these?" Molly asked. "Egyptian?"

"Maybe," Gabe said as he carefully used his flashlight to look over the details of one of the statues. "They have some Egyptian qualities, but there are also elements of them that look Chinese, Polynesian, possibly even Native American. I've never seen anything like it in any art I've ever studied."

"How could one piece of art have the influences of all those cultures?" Jarod asked. "It doesn't make sense does it?"

"In traditional terms—no, it makes no sense at all. But, if you're a proponent of the diffusionist school of history it makes perfect sense. These items may represent the earliest origins of human culture."

"This stuff has to be worth millions," Danny said.

"Try *billions*."

"That's great," Molly said impatiently. "But, I really don't care about this stuff—I just want to find Mark."

So, they continued to walk.

About an hour later, Gabe realized he had reached his limit. The dark dankness of the cave was becoming overwhelming, and he was exhausted.

"I'm sorry guys, but I have to stop and rest for a few minutes," he said.

None of the other of his three companions offered forth any argument; he had obviously just had said what everyone else had been thinking. They threw their packs down on the rock floor, and they sat on top of them.

Gabe directed his light around the area where they sat. There were still no discernible edges or ceiling to the current chamber.

"We should shut down all but one light while we're sitting here," Danny said. "We need to extend the battery life as much as possible. The further we go, the further we'll have to go back."

"How deep in are we?" Jarod asked.

Danny Kasa pulled out the GPS unit and studied it closely.

"Just slightly over three miles from the entrance."

"It's taken a long time to go three miles," Gabe said.

"Any walk seems long in the dark," Jarod replied.

Gabe opened his mouth to say something else, when he noticed Danny put his hand up signaling him to be quiet.

"Do you guys hear that?" he whispered.

Gabe listened closely. He had not noticed before, but he could now hear what Danny was talking about. There was some sort of sound coming from deeper in the cavern.

"I hear it," Jarod said.

"Me too," Molly added.

The four stood up and continued walking deeper into the cavern toward the sound that they all now heard. Their exhaustion from a few minutes ago had been replaced by the adrenalin of this new discovery.

They went about another hundred yards when they got the first glimpse of light coming from far in the distance. As they got closer, the light source continued to get larger and brighter. The lone light shone so brightly in the darkness that it took a full half mile of walking to get close to its source. The noise continued to get louder as well.

They came upon an arched opening in the stone wall. The sound and light was definitely coming from the space beyond it. They extinguished their lights and peered into the doorway. Just beyond there was ledge lined with large boulders that overlooked a large open area. They creeped out onto the ledge, hiding behind the large stones and peered into the space below.

"No fucking way," Molly said in a dramatic whisper.

Gabe said nothing, be he felt much the same way.

Below them was a huge open space, which resembled some sort of warehouse facility. There was a lot of heavy machinery, and probably two dozen men in what looked to be military uniforms. Far in the distance, Gabe could see a cargo truck driving in the opposite direction. As the truck moved, large overhead lights lit above it until it disappeared into the distance.

"What is this place?" Danny whispered.

"I'm not sure," Jarod replied. "But I think we found who set up that projection system outside."

"How are we going to get past them?" Molly asked.

"You're not."

All four jumped at the voice that came from behind them. They turned to face the speaker.

"Mr. Patrick, Agent Newman, Agent McIntire," a man in what appeared to be an officer's uniform said to them. "I for one never would have believed that you would make it this far."

Two other men in uniform stood behind him. The officer raised his hand in a gesture to move forward. As they did, Gabe saw that they were brandishing weapons that were pointed at him and his companions. Gabe noticed that the guns looked like nothing he had every seen before, and they were beginning to glow with an eerie green light.

Just then Gabe was hit with a massive shock like he had never felt before that seemed to vibrate through every cell in his body.

Then, everything went dark again.

CHAPTER 34

Unknown Location (Current Day)

Gabe was dreaming. Or, at least he hoped he was dreaming. He was stuck in a tunnel, watching a train with a bright light on its engine quickly bearing down on him. Then the train—and its light—abruptly disappeared.

"Pupils are responding," a distant voice said.

He had the sensation of being carried on some sort of gurney. He tried to move but he could not. He felt completely paralyzed. He opened his mouth to try to scream, but no sound would come out.

He felt a burning sensation in his arm. Then seconds later, everything went dark once again.

Gabe had only been diving a few times in his life, but he had always remembered the sensation of rising from the depths of the water to the surface; how the darkness of the deep gradually blended into light and clarity. He was far from water, but he was feeling that sensation right now.

He opened his eyes and tried to look around. He was in some sort of hospital bed, and there were sensors of some sort attached to his chest. He was in an otherwise empty room which he assumed must be some sort of medical facility. It was night and there were no lights on that he could see, but he could see light through a window on the other side of the room. He briefly realized that he was only wearing a tee shirt and some sort of scrub-type pants.

He had no idea how he had gotten here. The last thing he could remember was being in the cavern in the Grand Canyon. And, the military men with guns pointed at him.

He carefully removed the sensors attached to chest and pulled himself out of the bed. He stood up slowly as his feet hit the floor. If not for grabbing onto the railing on the side of the bed he would have fallen flat on the floor. Whatever they had given him—or done to him—had left him weak and light headed.

He walked slowly across the cold tile floor to the window on the other side of the room. He looked out the window into the dark night. He almost fell again as his mind struggled to comprehend what he was seeing in the distance.

It was a pyramid.

Just then the door to the room opened and a nurse entered.

"The subject in room four is conscious and mobile," she yelled out into the brightly lit hallway.

"Where have you taken me?" Gabe yelled at the woman. "What is going on?"

Two young burly men came rushing into the room to join her.

"Hold him while I administer the sedation," she told them.

Gabe tried to flee as the men reached forward to grab him, but there was no where to go. The men held him in a vice grip as the nurse prepared a hypodermic. He tried to fight them, but it was a lost cause.

Gabe felt a sharp stinging in his upper arm. Then, once again, everything went dark.

CHAPTER 35

Unknown Location (Current Day)

When Gabe awoke again he had no idea how much time had passed since his unpleasant experience with the nurse and her goons, but it had to be several hours at a minimum. While it had been night before, now bright sunshine was streaming into the room through the window.

Once again, he carefully extracted himself from the bed and slowly made his way across the floor to the window. He noticed now that the window glass was extremely thick, as if it was bullet proof. He looked out, and was faced again with the sight that had shocked him so much the night before.

A huge pyramid loomed in the distance.

To the left of the pyramid he could see the silhouette of the New York City skyline. Beyond that he could see the Eiffel Tower. Even further away was something that resembled Saint Marks in Venice.

It's fucking Vegas, he thought.

Just then the door to his room opened again, and two soldiers walked in. Gabe noticed that they were both armed, although both looked as though they were barely old enough to be out of high school.

"Sir," the slightly older looking of the two said. "You are to come with us by order of Colonel Latta."

"Sorry. Never heard of him."

He noticed both soldiers' hands went to their sidearms. He determined that trying to sound like a smart ass was not going to get him anywhere with these guys.

"Ok, guys. Lighten up," he said motioning with his arm. "After you."

He walked out of the room into the hallway with one of the young soldiers leading, and one following him. If this was a hospital, it was the strangest one he had ever seen. It looked more like an office building than a medical facility. What was even stranger is that it seemed to be completely empty other than himself and his chaperones.

After a few hundred feet down the hallway, the leading soldier stopped in front of a large, windowless steel door. Using his knuckles, he knocked three times hard on the door.

"Enter," a voice from the inside said.

The soldier opened the door, stood to the side and motioned for Gabe to enter. Gabe walked into the room, anxious about what might be waiting for him. But he was unbelievably happy to see who was waiting for him. Molly and Jarod were sitting in folding chairs facing away from him.

A man in an Army colonel's uniform was sitting on the edge of a desk facing them. There was a large mirror behind him. From the set up of the room, Gabe assumed they were in some sort of interrogation facility.

"Mr. Patrick," the officer said. "Happy to see you finally regained consciousness and were able to join us."

Both Molly and Jarod turned around at the mention of his name. Obviously as happy to see him as he was them.

"Have a seat," the officer said pointing to one of two empty seats next to Jarod and Molly.

Gabe sat down next to Molly. She grabbed a hold of his hand and squeezed it hard.

"So, first things first," the colonel said. "I can only assume he's the reason you trespassed on a top secret government facility."

He reached around and tapped the mirrored surface behind him. A second door next to the mirror opened. Mark Newman stepped through the door, squinting in an attempt to adjust to the brightly lit room.

"Mark!" Molly yelled, rising from her chair and running to hug him.

CHAPTER 36

Nevada Interrogation Center (Current Day)

After briefly allowing the heartfelt reunion between sister and brother, the military officer ordered all four of them back to their seats.

"I am Colonel Walter Latta with the National Security Agency. I oversee security at the Arizona facility that the four of you illegally entered."

"It was an honest mistake," Jarod said. "We got lost in the river, and…"

Colonel Latta quickly cut him off.

"Let's not insult each other's intelligence, Agent McIntire. We all know the truth of what you've done."

For the first time, Gabe realized that Danny Kasa was not with them.

"What have you done with Danny?"

"Mr. Kasa is a citizen of the Hopi nation, and as such has been turned over to his own tribal government to deal with. We're affording him a bit of…let's say, *diplomatic immunity*, in this situation."

Danny's three companions released a collective sigh of relief in the news that he was unharmed.

"Unfortunately," Latta continued. "Your situation won't have the same happy ending. The four of you illegally entered a top secret government facility considered critical to national defense. The fact that two of you are also Federal agents only makes that crime even more dire."

"I want to see an bureau attorney," Jarod said. "Now."

Colonel Latta laughed loudly.

"Oh, Agent McIntire. You really have no idea how much shit you've gotten you and your friends into, do you? This is no typical arrest; there will be no lawyers—there will be no trial. The full authority of the federal government has already determined your guilt, and the punishment will be fitting anyone who threatens the national security of the United States."

Gabe felt a near panic rush over him as he realized the full weight of what the colonel was saying to them. They were going to be sent to some terrible prison for the rest of their lives—or something even worse. His thoughts were interrupted by the ringing of a telephone sitting on the desk.

Colonel Latta also seemed surprised by the ringing phone, and stared at it for several seconds before picking up the receiver.

"What?" he said gruffly into the phone.

Gabe could hear an excited voice on the other end of the line, but could not discern any of the actual words being spoken.

"*Who?*" Latta said incredulously. "He's *here?* What in the hell is the Secretary of the Interior doing here?"

Gabe's ears perked up at the mention of Reginald Allard. He never thought in his life that he would welcome word of that man's arrival.

Just then, there was a sharp knock at the door Gabe had entered from the hallway. Without waiting for a response, the door opened and Reginald Allard entered with two armed U.S. Marshals of his own.

"Colonel Latta," Allard said. "I'm Secretary Allard, and I am here to take jurisdiction and possession of your guests."

CHAPTER 37

Nevada Interrogation Facility (Current Day)

It was clear that Colonel Latta was attempting to be respectful to this surprise visitor from the President's cabinet. However, it was equally clear he was seething with rage.

"Mr. Secretary, with all due respect you are drastically exceeding your authority here. The Park Service only has jurisdiction up to the threshold of the facility. Once inside, the NSA has full control."

Reginald Allard gave the man a slight smile, but said nothing in return. Once again, the desk phone started to ring.

"I think you'll want to take that call, Colonel," Allard said.

Latta looked even angrier, but he picked up the receiver.

"Colonel Latta," he said abruptly.

Gabe could hear another voice—lower this time—but once again could not discern any words. He saw the colonel's posture stiffen.

"Yes sir," he said. "Of course, sir."

Latta hung up the phone and looked directly at Reginald Allard.

"Secretary Allard, by the direct order of the President I am turning over custody of the four individuals to you. Good day."

With that, he saluted and motioned for his men to accompany him out of the room.

"Reg, what the hell is going on?" Gabe asked, but Allard raised his hand in a gesture for Gabe to stop talking.

"Marshals," Allard said to the armed men who came in with him. "Could I bother you to step out and give us the room for a moment?"

Both men nodded and walked out into the hallway, closing the large steel door behind them. Allard waited until the door was firmly closed, then he addressed Gabe directly.

"Well, well," Allard said with a smirk. "You really got in over your head this time, didn't you?"

"Reg—Mr. Secretary—you know we were looking for Molly's brother. We weren't trying to infiltrate any secret facility."

Allard laughed.

"Oh Gabe, of course I know that. I personally told the President of our conversation in my office. I had to cash in a few favors he owed me a little earlier than I expected to save your ass, but I figured it was worth it to have you in my debt."

At this point, being in Reginald Allard's debt was not the worst thing he could think of. He was just happy he would not be spending the rest of his life in some government prison.

"And," Allard continued. "I bet you four have a few questions about exactly what kind of facility you stumbled into."

All four looked at each other, surprised by the comment.

"I have been given authorization by the President personally to disclose certain points of information about the facility to you. I can give you the answers you came looking for, but you must accept responsibility for those answers."

"What does that mean?"

"It means that you'll be bound by the laws applicable to individuals given top secret information. You can never disclose that information, lest you'll be prosecuted for treason. You'd spend the rest of your life in Guantanamo—or some even worse place you've never heard of."

He paused for a moment to allow the gravity of his

words to register with his audience.

"Or," Allard continued. "You can forget about this whole episode and we'll put you on a transport back to Phoenix. The choice is yours."

"What makes you think we haven't already seen enough to take to the press?" Molly asked defiantly.

"Sure, you could do that. But there's already tons of ridiculous conspiracy theories about this subject on the internet—what's one more? But, that approach would seem like a waste of two very promising FBI careers…"

"I want to know the truth," Mark said quietly. "That's all I've ever really wanted."

"Me too," Gabe said.

Molly and Jarod nodded in agreement. They all wanted to know the truth—and would agree to accept Reginald Allard's conditions.

"Ok, then," Allard began. "If everyone is in agreement—let me tell you a little story. It all begins with an alcoholic con man who never realized he had stumbled into one of the greatest mysteries in human history…"

CHAPTER 38

Nevada Interrogation Facility (Current Day)

So, the article in the Phoenix Gazette was true?" Mark asked.

"The important parts, anyway."

Mark looked pleased. Gabe assumed it was the comfort of finally finding out that the theory he had spent years following had ultimately been proved correct. Of course, being right now also now meant that he would never be able to publish his doctoral dissertation on the subject.

"G.E. Kincaid was an old drunk that knew he had stumbled upon a very valuable treasure, but he lacked the means—and sobriety—to find a way to get back to recover it. He ended up spilling his guts to a newspaper reporter who published his story. That was a big mistake on his part."

"What happened to Kincaid?" Gabe asked.

"After the article was published and the Smithsonian

was planning an expedition, Theodore Roosevelt was approached by one of the major benefactors of the institution who requested he personally intervene to stop the expedition on the pretense of protecting an indigenous population."

Having read Julia Morgan's journals, Gabe understood exactly how that event came to occur. Julia Morgan had appealed to Charles Lang Freer who subsequently appealed to President Roosevelt. Since Reginald Allard had failed to mention her involvement in his retelling of the story, Gabe believed that her involvement in the official record must be unknown. For the sake of a woman that he never met—but greatly admired—that thought pleased Gabe very much.

Reginald Allard continued his narrative of the story.

"After stopping the expedition, Roosevelt started to believe there might be something of strategic value to the government out in the canyon, so he sent a military mission based on the plans the Smithsonian had put together. The army team found a treasure of immeasurable value."

"You never answered Gabe's question," Molly said. "What happened to Kincaid?"

"Kincaid was taken into custody for his own protection and unfortunately died shortly thereafter."

"Sure," Molly said. "For his own protection. Had nothing to do with keeping him quiet about the government's new found treasure, huh?"

Allard ignored the comment that was obviously dripping with sarcasm.

"They found more than just a priceless treasure, didn't they?" Gabe asked.

Allard smiled at him.

"Gabe, you've always been perceptive—I have to give you that," he said. "Yes, they found more than just treasure. They discovered a colony of people who had been living miles under ground for many, many years."

"People?" Jarod asked. "What kind of people."

"That's a great question, Agent McIntire. Unfortunately, I can't provide a definitive answer on that."

"You can't provide an answer," Mark said. "Because the government never actually solved that part of the mystery."

"That would be an accurate statement. These people were so much more technically advanced than anything that had ever been seen before, that the researchers at the time could barely make heads or tails of anything about them."

"How many people did they find?" Gabe asked.

"Not many—a few dozen perhaps."

"Where are they now?" Mark asked.

"Dead. All of them."

Gabe shuddered at the thought. Julia Morgan's

biggest fear for the people she found honor bound to protect had come true.

"Who were they?" Jarod asked. "Indians? Some long lost offshoot of the Navajo or Hopi?"

"Again, I can't provide a definite answer on that. Two of the bodies were preserved and DNA testing was done on them a few years ago. But, it was inconclusive."

"Inconclusive?" Gabe asked.

"Yes. The remains were definitely human, but with no discernible ethnicity. The geneticists who conducted the studies actually declared them to be a completely new ethnic race. But, researchers on the very early expeditions had taken to calling them *the Spanish*."

"The Spanish?" Molly asked. "Why would they call them that?"

"It actually started as a really bad joke. There was a lot of discussion among the teams early about the ethnicity of the people, but with no definite answers. The people were darker complected, but with eyes much, much larger than normal—probably evolved over time to accommodate the darkness underground. In one of the many discussions about their origins, one of the Army officers reportedly said *'maybe they're some kind of Spanish or something.'* A racist comment certainly, but the name stuck."

"Why were only two bodies preserved?" Gabe asked.

"You said that there were a few dozen people present when the colony was encountered."

"It was considered far too dangerous after what happened in 1918…"

Reginald Allard paused for what Gabe could only assume was dramatic effect. As usual, he was enjoying being the center of attention.

"In early 1918 the people from the cavern started to get sick—very sick. One by one, they began dying. The government physicians tried to save them, but medical science at that time was not nearly advanced enough to be effective with such an unknown and deadly disease. We had even less understanding of communicable diseases, and that lack of understanding proved to be devastating and very deadly."

"The Spanish Flu," Gabe said.

"Yes, the great worldwide flu pandemic of 1918 can be directly traced to our encounter with this mysterious tribe of people living the Grand Canyon. One of the physicians who had visited the site had returned to his home in Kansas not realizing he had been infected with the disease. He became sick and died, but not before he had already spread the disease to others. By the time the pandemic had run its course, one hundred million people—basically six percent of the world's population at the time—were dead."

Gabe looked around at his companions. He was sure the looks of shock and disbelief on their faces accurately reflected how they were processing this bizarre story that the Secretary of the Interior was telling to them.

"After that, the government got a lot more careful about quarantining the facility. All but two of the Spanish died during the flu epidemic. All of the corpses were burned to try to prevent further spreading of the virus."

"What happened to the remaining two?" Mark asked.

"They lived for several more years, although they changed dramatically after their companions died. Early on, they seemed to actively engage with the government scientists—trying to communicate and it even seemed if they were trying to help us understand their technology. But, after their compatriots died they seemed to completely disengage."

"When did they die?" Gabe asked.

"The first died in 1942. No cause was ever determined, and many wondered if he had somehow taken his own life. The United States was in the throes of World War Two, and was looking for any advantage they could find over the Germans and Japanese. With only one of the mysterious tribe members left they knew time was running out to have their help to interpret the mysteries of the cavern. For the first time, the decision was made to remove one of the Spanish from the underground complex in the Grand

Canyon and bring him to Washington for focused study."

"What happened to him?" Molly asked quietly, fearing she already knew the answer.

"He died within minutes of being brought to the surface. Apparently, they had grown so accustomed to living deep below the Earth that they could not survive when removed from that environment."

"You mentioned that we attempted to communicate with them—what language did they speak?" Jarod asked.

"Linguists have never been able to fully classify it. They way they communicated with each other was not a language in the traditional sense—it was an odd combination of spoken words, mathematical symbols, and even telepathy. Einstein was able to interpret some of the mathematical components when he was brought in for consulting. And, some children could seem to understand portions of the communication—although, they all lost the ability by the age of ten or so."

Molly sighed loudly. Gabe knew her well enough to know that the limits of her patience had pretty much been reached.

"How do we know this isn't just all a bunch of bullshit?" she asked.

"I guess you don't. But, I think the results of the work and research the government has done with the facility in the canyon speaks for itself."

"What do you mean?" Gabe asked.

"Has it never seemed strange to you that the world entered the twentieth century living by candlelight and traveling by equine and cart, yet ended the century using super computers and visiting alien worlds? At no time in the history of the planet has society progressed so far, so fast."

"And," Jarod said. "You'd have us believe that's all due to some mysterious colony of people living inside the Grand Canyon."

"You can believe whatever you want, but you said you wanted to know the truth and I agreed to tell it to you."

"If we weren't able to communicate with these people," Gabe asked. "How have we been able to take advantage of their technology?"

"It's been a very slow process of reverse engineering, involving some of the world's greatest scientists, engineers, and technologists. Some discoveries have been more valuable than others—the microchip, for instance, was of particular benefit."

"I know that's a load of crap," Jarod said. "An engineer by the name of Jack Kilby at Texas Instruments invented the microchip."

"Actually, Agent McIntire, Jack Kilby and another engineer from Fairfield Semiconductor named Robert Noyce share *credit* for the invention. However, they were provided some special assistance, by virtue of the people in the canyon."

"So," Gabe said. "The government just gave away this technology?"

"Not really gave it away, but rather helped funnel certain information to various individuals and groups which showed particular promise in certain areas," Reginald Allard said. "Sort of the government sanctioned version of *helping those who help themselves.*"

Gabe realized that Mark had said very little during Reginald Allard's outrageous tale. Maybe his years of studying the mystery in the canyon enabled him to be more open minded than his companions.

"As much as the discoveries in the canyon have enabled human kind to progress so quickly, there's still much, much more to be realized. Some things have been reverse engineered—like the energy weapons that rendered you unconscious in the cavern—but have not yet been integrated into society. There are some things mankind just isn't ready for—yet."

"There's one thing that perplexes me about all this, Reg," Gabe said. "How in the world do you know all of this? I can't think this was a subject that was covered in the first day of your cabinet orientation program."

Reginald Allard laughed loudly.

"You always have dramatically underestimated me, Gabe," Allard said. "Since the facility is located in the middle of a national park, part of its security is under the jurisdiction of the Department of the Interior. It may have seemed like you waltzed right into the secret cave, but you all were under surveillance pretty much from the moment you left my office in Washington."

He paused for a moment, looked at Mark, then added:

"You too, Mr. Newman. You can't make as many inquiries about the mystery in the canyon as you did and not raise some governmental red flags. All of you were able to enter the facility because you were allowed to enter the facility."

Gabe noticed the look of indignation Mark directed at Reginald Allard. Gabe imagined that the Secretary noticed it as well.

"After Gabe showed up in Washington asking for my help to obtain the canyon permits, I got curious. I knew about the role my agency had in the security of that area of the Grand Canyon, so I decided to get some more information. The President's chief-of-staff is a former director of the CIA, so I was confident he could provide the information I was looking to obtain."

"And, the chief-of-staff was willing to just share top secret information with you?" Jarod asked.

"Well, keep in mind—I am eighth in line to Presidential succession, so that affords me a certain level of clearance," Reginald Allard said with a wink. "Plus, let's just say that I have some personal knowledge of the chief-of-staff that encouraged him to tell me what I wanted to know."

Gabe felt a strange comfort in the realization that his negative feelings toward this man had always been justified. He was a sanctimonious prick when he had worked for him at Ohio State, and he still was today.

"Ok," Molly said. "Let's assume this is a true story. But, I work for the federal government, and trust me—I've have not witnessed the kind of competence that would be needed to keep a thing like this secret."

"Oh Agent Newman, you should have more faith in the organizations which employ you. The United States government can be very good about keeping a secret safe when it needs to be."

Mark laughed sarcastically, and Reginald Allard stared at him.

"Yeah, right," Mark said. "Just like Area 51, huh?"

Then, it was Allard's turn to laugh out loud.

"People believe the conspiracy theories about Area 51, Roswell, and a host of other things because that's what they are intended to believe. If just enough encouragement is provided, conspiracy theorists will spend all their time chasing their tails on those stories. All the while a much bigger—and much more shocking—truth is happening all around them."

Gabe had no idea whether or not the story that had been told to them was true or not. However, at that moment, he believed that if nothing else Reginald Allard certainly believed it. And, that meant something to him.

"So, Reg," Gabe said. "What's your scientific opinion on this lost tribe of mysterious people? Where did they come from?"

Allard looked at him with pleasant surprise, pleased at the genuine tone of professional respect in his former colleague's query. For once, he decided to return the sentiment.

"Honestly, Gabe—I don't know. Even after over a hundred years of study, I don't think anyone does or maybe ever will. We're confident that their society is very, very old. Remnants and artifacts of every culture known to man throughout the entire course of human history—and several we've never been able to identify—have been found within their underground world."

He paused, for a moment then continued:

"Maybe man isn't meant to understand the true

nature of his origin."

With that, Reginald Allard fell silent. He had told them all that he knew, and all that he was authorized to tell.

"So, that's the whole story," Allard said. "That's what you risked your lives and freedom to find out."

"It was worth it," Mark said.

Reginald Allard nodded. At heart, he was still a scholar and a scientist and he was prone to agree with the young man.

"I must remind you again that you have been given specific clearance to hear this information, and the laws regarding top secret information fully apply. Any leaking of this information would be considered treason, and you would suffer the consequences."

He paused, again Gabe assumed for dramatic effect, then added:

"Not even the person eighth in line to the presidency could save your asses then."

After Reginald Allard had finished his story, Gabe and his companions were given back their clothes and other items they had with them when they were captured in the cavern complex in the Grand Canyon. A plane belonging to the National Parks Service would transport them from Las Vegas back to Phoenix.

Reginald Allard had personally accompanied them to the small landing strip outside of town where they would catch the plane. After the other three had entered the small aircraft, Allard stopped Gabe and told him that he wanted to speak to him for a few moments alone.

"I hope you realize that the balance between us is no longer even."

"What do you mean?"

"I mean, that you owe me now. I not only saved the lives of you and your friends, but provided all of the answers that you sought. And, I did so at great personal and professional risk to myself."

"Ok. So, what do you want, Reg?"

"I don't know yet. But, you're a smart, talented guy and I have no doubt that sometime in the future you're going to be in a position to help me. And, I'm going to fully expect you to provide that help—without hesitation—when I ask for it."

Gabe looked directly at him, but said nothing in response.

"Are we clear, Gabe?"

"We're clear."

"Excellent. You and your friends have a good trip

back to Arizona, and you back to Columbus."

Reginald Allard offered his hand as a parting gesture. Gabe's immediate reaction was to ignore the handshake, or make some other more profane demonstration. But then he heard the words of his late mentor Rudolph Zeffner clearly in his mind.

Liebchen, you must learn how to play the game.

Gabe shook Reginald Allard's hand, then turned and walked up the boarding stairs of the waiting plane.

CHAPTER 39

Arizona State University Medical Center (Current Day)

Until today, Gabe had never believed in the concept of love at first sight.

But, as he stood at the nursery window and watched the newborn Zachary Daniel Newman through the glass, he believed he finally understood what that meant.

Molly had been unable to reach Vickie after their cell phones had been returned to them when they were released from custody. Worried, Molly contacted a close friend of their's who said Vickie had been rushed to the hospital several hours earlier with labor pains.

As soon as the plane landed in Phoenix they went immediately to the ASU Medical Center, escorted by the U.S. Marshals who had brought them back to Arizona. Molly made it into the delivery room just fifteen minutes before

Vickie gave birth to their baby boy.

Molly joked with Gabe later that she was kind of happy to have missed the previous twenty five hours of labor and got to show up just in time for the good part. Gabe suggested that for her own good she not make that same joke within earshot of Vickie.

Now he stood there staring at the child he helped bring into the world, and it all seemed so surreal—wonderful, but surreal.

Gabe was startled to feel a hand on his shoulder, and then heard a voice behind him.

"He's a good looking kid. Just like his dad."

Gabe turned around and faced Jarod, smiling widely.

"Thanks, but I think I'll be more like a favorite uncle—after all, he already has two parents."

"Well, whatever you'll be to him," Jarod said. "He'll be one lucky kid to have you in his life."

"Did you notice that Vickie and Molly gave him the middle name of Daniel?" Gabe asked. "I guess Danny Kasa made a great impression."

"Yeah, I told him that when he called," Jarod said. "He was thrilled."

"Danny called?"

"Yeah, he was frantic after the Feds returned him to the Hopi council. He was sure we were going to end up in some secret Federal prison. Betty Honantewa was already organizing a huge protest in Washington to make everyone aware of our plight. I guess we gave her the inspiration to return to her old radical ways."

Gabe laughed at the comment.

"I have a feeling those radical ways were always just under the surface anyway," he said. "How are you going to get the Range Rover back?"

"Danny and some of his friends went out into the desert and picked it up for me. It's just waiting for me to pick it up in Old Oraibi. In fact, Betty asked if we could come up this weekend to pick up the SUV and have dinner. I didn't know how soon you were heading back to Ohio, and I didn't want to speak for you…"

"I think I could stick around for a few more days," Gabe said interrupting, and wanting to relieve Jarod of his discomfort. "Besides, I imagine Molly and Vickie will need some help with the baby in the beginning anyway."

Jarod smiled, obviously pleased with Gabe's response.

The two stood in front of the nursery window silently for a few moments, just watching the baby sleep. A nurse smiled at them from the other side, and held baby Zachary up so that they could have a better look.

"So, holding all these secrets about the mysterious origins of the world must be quite a burden," Jarod finally said.

Gabe turned and looked at him, somewhat confused.

"Molly told me about the murder of your old friend, and how you and Kevin were nearly killed trying to retrieve the Tzohar," Jarod continued. "To be honest, I'd never heard of the Tzohar before—but it's got quite a story on Wikipedia."

Gabe smiled at him. He assumed Molly's opinion of Jarod must definitely have changed over the past few days if she were willing to confide something so personal to him.

"A week ago I never would have believed it. But, over the last few days I think I've become much more open minded about the mysteries of the universe."

"Well," Gabe said. "Open minded is a good thing."

Jarod nodded and smiled.

"So, do you want to go grab some coffee or something? I haven't had any real caffeine since that night at Betty's. There's a Starbucks just down the street."

"Yeah, that would be great."

As they walked toward the exit of the hospital, Gabe felt Jarod take his hand in his and squeeze it firmly. He squeezed back. At that moment, Gabe was sure he would not have been able to stop smiling even if his life would have depended upon it.

Then the automatic doors swooshed open, and they slipped into the cool desert evening together.

AUTHOR NOTES

One of my favorite parts of a novel like this (aside from the story itself, of course) are the end notes where the author explains which parts of the book are complete fiction, and which parts are based on fact. Since you've read this far, I assume you have a similar interest in separating the truth (or, mostly truth) from fantasy.

First off, a story really did appear on the front page of the *Phoenix Gazette* on April 5, 1909. The article told the amazing story of a Mr. G.E. Kinkaid and his miraculous discovery of Egyptian treasure hidden inside a deep cave somewhere within the Grand Canyon. The individuals mentioned in this novel from the newspaper article (Kinkaid, Professor Jordan of the Smithsonian, etc.) are actual names listed in the story as published in 1909. A quick web search using the term "Egyptian treasure in the Grand Canyon" will provide numerous links to the text of the actual *Phoenix Gazette* article on the Internet.

Passages from the article listed in the early chapters are repeated verbatim from the text of the 1909 newspaper story. Although, I did change the spelling of the protagonist's surname from "Kinkaid" in the article to the more standard spelling of "Kincaid."

While some descriptions of G.E. Kincaid in the novel are based on information listed about him in the article (including his claim of being the "first white child born in Idaho"), nearly all of his back story was fabricated as part of this story. In fact, there's no indication (other than this single newspaper story) that a G.E. Kincaid (or "Kinkaid" for that matter) ever even existed. There are many articles on the web written by people who have attempted to research the story only to find no proof of Kinkaid, and denials by the Smithsonian of ever planning the expedition to the Grand Canyon, or employing a Dr. S.A. Jordan.

As expected, the lack of concrete evidence of the main characters in the article, and an outright denial by a government institution has only served to fuel conspiracy and cover-up theories on the topic. I really have no opinion on these presumed conspiracies one way or another, however I thought it all fed very nicely into this story.

Julia Morgan was a noted California architect of the

early twentieth century, and served as William Randolph Hearst's favorite architect for a large portion of her career. While *La Cuesta Encantada* was one of their most noted collaborations, Julia Morgan was the primary architect of record on over seven hundred buildings throughout the Western United States. She is considered one of the most important architects of her time, which for a woman in the early 1900s—is quite an impressive feat.

Most of her background related in the novel is true, regarding her family, education, career and personal life. With, however, the notable exception of her life defining event in the novel which occurred while lost in the Grand Canyon. That entire part of the story was concocted entirely for the purposes of this book.

Interestingly, one of the passages in the novel related to Julia Morgan that *sounds* the most fictional is actually based on truth according to a biography written about her. In a book called *Julia Morgan Architect* by Sara Holmes Boutelle (1988), that author reports that Julia Morgan really did request that her longtime personal assistant burn all of her files, blueprints, office records and personal correspondence on the day she closed her office in the Merchants Exchange Building. However, in real life her personal assistant's name was actually Otto Haake. I renamed him Walter Hake and created his fictional grandson (Trevor) for the story. It can only be assumed that the real Otto actually followed Miss Morgan's wishes and burned all of her papers as requested on that last day of work (unlike the actions taken by his fictional counterpart, Walter Hake).

The tale of the Freer Museum and its benefactor are for the most part factual. Charles Lang Freer really did battle with the director of the Smithsonian over the control of "his" museum, and really did go over the man's head, directly appealing to President Theodore Roosevelt. (Who, obviously, took Mr. Freer's side in the argument.) However, I have no reason to believe that Charles Lang Freer and Julia Morgan ever met. The meeting described in Detroit (and the gift of an amulet to Freer's collection and subsequent second appeal to Roosevelt) is pure fiction.

I have tried to be as accurate as possible when describing specific locations in the book, right down to things like driving distances and other mundane trivia. I have actually visited many of the locales in the novel so many of the observations are based on my own experience and memory. In situations where I did not personally experience the location or situation (for instance, I've never traveled by raft through the Grand Canyon), I relied on reading photographic travel journals of others who had made such journeys, and experiencing them vicariously through other people clearly more adventurous than myself.

I enjoyed telling this story, and I am happy that in the end it was able to provide some answers for Gabe and his friends, yet still maintaining some mystery in the bigger picture of human history and our shared culture.

There is a quote from Reginald Allard toward the end of the novel that I think best sums it all up best for me:

Maybe man isn't meant to understand the true nature of his origin.

ACKNOWLEDGEMENTS

I started off the acknowledgements of my first novel by mentioning the long held belief of most authors that no one writes a book alone. I can only say that I believe that more strongly now than I even did then.

I was absolutely amazed at the wonderful support I received after the publication of *Chasing the Light*. Not only from friends, family, and colleagues, but also from people who I didn't even know. There are few things I can think of more humbling than receiving an email from someone you never met, and have them tell you something profound about a character you created that you had never realized yourself; some personal way that the character or story had affected them. I was familiar with developing connections to characters in books as a reader, but I had never experienced it from the standpoint of a writer. Quite simply, it made me finally understand the real reason why authors write.

I want to thank Scott, Jessica, and Jim for serving as my early reading focus group and providing the all important feedback and edits. After publication of the first novel, I truly came to believe that Jessica had missed her professional calling—she should have been a publicist and book agent! She encouraged me into marketing approaches I never would have felt comfortable going into on my own, and I sincerely appreciate all of her help.

This is not only Jim's second stint as one of my editors, but he also loaned his last name to one of the major characters in this novel. I liked the character of Reginald Allard; not quite a bad guy, but not yet quite a good guy either. He was complex and interesting, and I thought a worthy namesake for my friend Jim. (And, Reginald also provides a great foray into the third novel…).

I dedicated this book to my good friends Dee Dee and Julie who have been my friends for nearly my entire life. We spent our childhood together, yet when we get together it's like no years at all have passed. Other than family, there are maybe a handful of people in the entire world who I know will always be with me—Dee Dee and Julie are two of them.

Finally, I finish these acknowledgements in the same way as my first novel—by thanking my partner Scott. As they sing in the theme song from my favorite Pixar movie:

I wouldn't have nothin' if I didn't have you.

ABOUT THE AUTHOR

Joel Zarley has wanted to be a writer his entire life. And, after writing two novels, he's finally starting to feel a little more like one.

As a journalism major at The Ohio State University, he followed an interest in writing and communications and has enjoyed a corporate "day job" in the career of workplace training and development.

He resides in Columbus with his partner and is currently working on his third novel which will continue the Gabriel Patrick *Lost Loves* series.

His website is www.purplepalmmedia.com.